The Sleepless Nights of Leah Bontrager A Collection of Amish Romance

Hannah Winstone

Published by Trellis Publishing, 2021.

This is a work of fiction. Similarities to real people, places, or events are entirely coincidental.

THE SLEEPLESS NIGHTS OF LEAH BONTRAGER A COLLECTION OF AMISH ROMANCE

First edition. July 1, 2021.

ISBN: 979-8224451661

Written by Hannah Winstone.

THE SLEEPLESS NIGHTS OF LEAH BONTRAGER

HANNAH WINSTONE

THE SLEEPLESS NIGHTS OF LEAH BONTRAGER
AMISH VALLEY
AMISH AMITY
JOANNA
FANNIE : AN AMISH WIDOW
RECKLESSLY AMISH
AMISH HIDEAWAY

Bleary eyes blinked open, slender hands reached out to grab for the old fashioned clock sitting on the ancient side table. It was still dark, the world beyond her thin cotton curtains swallowed up by the night. So why was she awake?

Leah Bontrager lived alone with her seven year old daughter, Elizabeth - and that meant *everything* was a worry. Already her heart rate had picked up, anxiety settling in the pit of her stomach. Swinging her legs over the bed she stood, fumbling in the dark for her robe.

That was when the first *patter patter* of footsteps reached her ears, echoing up the stairs and along the hall. Someone was in her living room. Not Elizabeth, because it was four in the morning and because Elizabeth's footsteps weren't nearly so heavy. A loud *clang* emanated from downstairs, followed by hushed cussing, and Leah thought herself lucky to be such a light sleeper.

There was no house phone upstairs and Leah, being Amish, had no cell. With creeping unease, she realised she had two choices. Stay upstairs and hope the burglar left without anything important - or go downstairs and confront them herself.

She was already reaching for the rifle her late husband insisted she kept. The law stated the ammo be kept in a safe - and truth be told she didn't *have* any anyway. Stomach rolling, she hoped the threat was enough.

The heavy, thudding footsteps rang in her ears. Were they getting closer?

In the next few moments, Leah didn't think - if she allowed herself to do so, surely she would have backed down, realised the danger of what she was doing. But she didn't think, and instead crept down the carpeted stairs with the rifle clasped in shaking hands.

A shadow moved in the corner of her eyes. It shifted and twisted, like something from a nightmare - but it was only the kitchen curtains flowing in the breeze from an opened window.

Oh. That *definitely* hadn't been open when she went to bed.

Pushing forward, Leah fought back the urge to be sick.

Another shadow twisted in the kitchen, but this one was *human*. One thick arm gripped a knife, glinting in the weak moonlight. Leah's foot hit a creaky floorboard and she winced, silently cursing her own carelessness - and the man spun, lurched forward with the knife forward.

Then his face hit the weak light and she caught sight of deep set grey eyes and the pale, lined face of someone old beyond they're years. Worst of all she *recognised him,* recognised the blue tint to that deep, charcoal grey, recognised they dark mop of black hair.

But who *was he?*

Leah had no time to think. She sprang back as he advanced, a gasp caught in her throat - and brandished the rifle. "Get *out* of my house!" she demanded in a hissing whisper. Upstairs remained silent, and Leah sent a prayer that Elizabeth remained asleep. Remained oblivious.

The man didn't speak - and somehow it was *worse* than the knife in his hand and worse than the unnerving glint in his dark eyes. He hesitated, however, eyeing the rifle as if considering his options. Whether he truly believed she was a threat was impossible to know - his face was *blank,* completely unreadable save for the downward quirk of his thin lips.

"I mean it," she warned, voice low, "get out of my house or I'll shoot." Her slender fingers teased the trigger - and only *she* knew it was empty inside. Blue eyes narrowed, lips pursed - and despite her short stature she hoped she conveyed the intimidating presence she was so desperate for.

The man's fists clenched - but he glared at the knife in his hands as if realising it was no match for a gun. Then he *snarled,* the sound chilling Leah to the bone - and pushed past her with enough force she tumbled into the wall.

By the time she had picked herself up, wild eyes darting across the room, he was gone. The curtains flapped gently in the wind, but everything else was perfectly still. She stood there, dazed, heart hammering - and then bolted for the phone.

She hadn't expected an answer at such a ridiculous time - but then the dial tone cut off and a man's sleepy voice answered, "Sheriff's office. How can I help?"

"Eli - uh, Sherrif?"

"That's me."

Leah hadn't heard his voice in *years,* not since they were both teenagers and he liked to hang out near the bakery her mother owned. His voice, rich and smooth, calmed her immediately. Even so, her voice shook as she said, "it's Leah Bontrager. Someone... someone broke into my house just now."

Eli jumped to attention then - and she just pictured him bolting up in his seat, eyes wide. "Right now? Are they still there? I'll be over immediately-"

"I chased them off," Leah assured, "Jesse's rifle finally came in useful." She laughed then, a tiny strained sound that sounded exhausted even to her own ears.

Eli breathed in relief. "Thank God. Is your daughter okay? Her name is... Eliza, right?"

"Elizabeth," Leah corrected without malice. They hadn't seen each other in so long, long before she was married. How could she expect him to know? "She's all right - still asleep, I hope."

"Then you go see to her. I'll be over as soon as I can, I promise."

"Thank you," Leah murmured. The clunky, ancient phone shook in her hands - and even though no one was there to see her, Leah swiped at her eyes before tears had the chance to fall. She had to get a hold of herself before Eli arrived. Letting out a hollow breath she added, "can you hurry?"

"I doubt he'll come back - but yes, of course."

Hanging up on Eli left her hollow, too exhausted to even worry any more. She stood there for a moment, ears straining to listen for anything unusual, anything *wrong* - and then she made the trek upstairs to make sure her daughter was okay.

———————————

The next morning, after all was said and done, Leah was surprised to find Sheriff Eli Jones on her doorstep at twenty-past nine in the morning. She greeted him with a smile and a confused quirk of her brow - but let him inside without hesitation. "Not that I'm complaining of course," she mentioned, "but why are you here?"

Eli cast a glance into the living room - where Elizabeth played, toys scattered across the carpet. "I have news about the break in," he whispered.

That drew her attention. Although she doubted Elizabeth could hear - or was even listening - she led Eli into the kitchen. Once the door was firmly closed behind them both she asked, "you do? Good news, I hope."

Eli collapsed heavily into the closest dining chair. He was a sturdy man - tall and broad, with strong muscle hidden under his Sheriff's uniform - but in that moment he looked so *small*. "Not exactly," he admitted with a sigh, "there hasn't been a break in or burglary in this area in over six years. This is a respectable neighbourhood, doesn't usually need my intervention."

Settling down on the rickety chair across from him, Leah silently urged him to continue. She didn't like where this was going - but she *needed* to know. For the safety of not just herself but her daughter, too.

"I don't think this *was* an attempted burglary," he revealed. Eli shook his head as if to physically dispel the negative thoughts, dark curls flopping in his face. It was cute, actually - a lot cuter than the awful, unkempt hair she remembered as a teen. "He didn't take anything - as far as we can tell, he didn't even *try* to take anything."

"I caught him before he could," Leah reminded with a forced laugh, although her stomach twisted uneasily.

Eli regarded her with dark hazel eyes, thick brows furrowed. She had never seen him so *careful,* so unsure of his own words. The Eli she remembered was brash and honest no matter what. "Something doesn't add up," he admitted eventually, "I just can't figure out *what*. And with no evidence..."

"You can't even prove anyone was here."

He nodded, head ducked in embarrassment. Leah almost swore he *flushed,* but perhaps it was just the dim lighting making her see things. "I don't want to overreact," he answered hesitantly, "but I want you to be extra careful. Keep the doors and windows locked, and keep that rifle close by. Call me if anything - and I mean *anything* - unusual happens."

He's just being a good Sheriff, Leah reasoned with herself - but it didn't stop the dopey grin that spread across her full lips, or the dusting of pink that spread across her already rosy cheeks. "Thank you, Eli," she replied with a soft sigh - only to flush scarlet as she realised what she had called him. Not Sheriff, but *Eli.* She hadn't had the right to call him that since they were teenagers.

Not that he seemed to mind, and his bright smile made her stomach untwist. "I'll keep working on this, I promise. He won't get away with this."

Her entire torso bloomed with warmth, as did her cheeks. Leah only hoped it was still early - and dim - enough he couldn't see the way she blushed like a school kid. "I appreciate it, Eli. I just wish we had reunited under better circumstances."

"I've been Sheriff here for five years," he reminded her, but not unkindly, "we've had plenty of chances to talk. But after so many years I... well, I supposed I figured you had moved on, grown out of our friendship."

They had been friends throughout childhood, ever since Leah's parents took over the little bakery on the street corner across from his home. Although home schooled, Leah had loved playing with the other children in the neighbourhood - but Eli had always been her favourite. Times had changed. They weren't kids any more, and Leah had a daughter of her own to think about. That didn't mean she was any less grateful to have Eli here, sitting in her own kitchen like a pillar of support.

Leah wasn't even aware as she leaned across the table to clasp his thick hands in her own delicate ones. She squeezed gently, smiling when he reciprocated. "You're here now, and so am I. Maybe once this is all over we could get coffee together, catch up on lost time?"

He *beamed,* and that bright smile lit up the entire room. "I'd enjoy that," he replied, voice thick with sincerity, "but for now, let's focus on keeping you and Elizabeth safe."

"Yeah," Leah breathed. It was in that moment that she realised her hands still held his - and she drew them back, shoving them deep in the pockets of her dress with a nervous little laugh. "Thanks for stopping by," she spoke - *too quickly,* she chastised mentally - and hopped to her feet. "You have *no* idea how glad I am that you're here."

She never would have predicted that Eli would pull her in for a hug - but he *did,* thick arms wrapping around her shoulders as he tugged her close. She relaxed into his warmth and her arms timidly wrapped around his waist. It felt intimate - perhaps *too* intimate after so long apart - but it didn't matter.

When Eli finally pulled away Leah found herself wanting to stop him, wanting to tug him back into the embrace. Instead she stood back, heat rushing to her round face, and said, "stop by whenever you want, Eli - and not just for work."

"I'll see you soon, Leah."

She hovered by the front door long after he had gone, hopping from foot to foot restlessly. It wasn't until Elizabeth called for her that she tore herself away, letting the door slip closed behind her.

————————————

Leah fumbled with the key to the bakery. After her mother had retired the little shop was left to her, and Leah had dutifully kept the business going ever since. It was barely light outside, the sky still dull and thick with clouds; but fresh goods needed to be baked - not to mention she was grateful for the normalcy of it all.

The door swung open and she edged inside, fumbling for the light switch. The lights flickered on and the kitchen swam into view. Pristine counters lined the far wall, her baking station exactly how she had left it. Yes, it was a little modern for her tastes - but with the town growing and other bakeries popping up all over, Leah had to improvise to stay afloat.

In the early morning the bakery was still, silent except for her boots on the tiled kitchen floor. She loved this time of morning - peaceful and quiet, it was easy to forget everything that had happened.

Until she wandered into the tiny sitting area by the display. The front door - the one customer's used - was still locked up tight, but something thin and white had been slipped under the gap. It was bright white against the dark wood of the floor. Brows scrunched, Leah scooped it up. A letter? The envelope had no address or name, no sign of who it came from *or* who it was for.

Peeling it open, Leah found herself sweating. Her hands shook as she unfolded the paper inside - and then with a deep breath, she read.

You might have escaped me once, but it won't happen again. Watch out, Leah.

Her hands slipped and the paper drifted to the floor as she stumbled back. Dark eyes snapped wide, darting from the letter to the door - and then to the kitchen. Her heart skipped as she imagined someone revealing themselves right there, appearing from one of the dozens of hiding places within the little bakery.

But no one appeared, wielding a knife or otherwise. Leah was completely alone.

She stumbled back into the kitchen with tears in her eyes. Although she blinked them away a few still escaped the corner of her eyes, splashing against the fabric of her coat. It took less than thirty seconds for her hands to close over the phone and dial, but it felt like an *eternity.*

"Sheriff's office-"

"Eli, it's Leah. You were right - I don't think it was just a burglary. I found a letter today - he knows where I *work*.. Elizabeth is with her grandmother - what if he knows where she is? What if-"

"Leah," his voice, always so *soothing* and sweet, melted through her panic. "I'll come over immediately. Are you at the bakery?"

"Yes."

"Stay there." Static followed the sound of hasty movement, no doubt as Eli scrabbled to grab what he needed. "I'll be there in ten minutes."

"Thank you," Leah breathed. The phone clicked off but she stood there for what could have been *hours,* clutching it to her chest as if it was the only thing keeping her tethered.

She snapped back to reality with a jolt when a shrill knock pierced her ears. She spun, gasping - until she heard Eli's gentle voice calling for her. Grabbing the keys, she let him in.

He wasted no time in rushing to her, wrapping thick arms around her waist and tugging her close. "Are you okay?" he questioned softly - and Leah couldn't help but sink into his warmth. "Did you see him again?"

She shook her head, and then buried it firmly in the crook of his shoulder. "No, the letter was already there. I-it was a threat of some kind, but I don't know *why.* I don't even know who he is or what he wants."

"We'll figure it out," Eli murmured against her skin. Once, Leah would have shied away from such affection - it simply wasn't appropriate, especially for two people who hadn't seen each other in over ten years. Yet she found herself sinking further into his embrace, eyes slipping closed - and Eli wasn't shy to reciprocate, tightening his thick arms around her.

Eventually they had to part, and the loss of contact left her cold despite the thick coat still clinging to her small frame. "I'll uh, get you the letter," she muttered, head lowered as her cheeks glowed.

"I'll get it. By the entrance?" Eli questioned. He hovered for a moment after she confirmed, as if afraid to leave her alone for even a second - but then he trudged through to pick it up from where she had abandoned it.

By the time Eli had moved back to the kitchen, his face had paled. "This *is* a threat," he confirmed, "which strengthens my theory." His eyes flickered up, and it was impossible to miss the frown that graced his features.

Leah wasn't sure if she wanted him to continue or not.

He leaned against the nearest counter, but he was so tall it barely reached his waist. "Years ago there was a string of murders - all unmarried women with kids. Well, specifically *one* child; usually a girl but not always. We... we never caught the murderer, even after it was handed over to state police."

Leah swallowed thickly. Her dark eyes darted down to her hands - which had been pulling at a loose thread on her sleeve. It snapped off in her hands and she dropped it to the floor. "You think it's the same guy?"

A sigh escaped from Eli's lips - lips which she was so used to seeing *smile,* even in the toughest situations. It only made her anxiety rise as he said, "honestly, I don't know for sure - but we can check this letter for fingerprints and the like, get the police in on this."

"Thanks, Eli." Leah surprised herself by diving in for another hug - and he was so *warm* and *inviting* that her racing heartbeat immediately calmed. She pressed her cheek to the side of his neck, inhaling the scent of cigarettes and coffee. Not an appealing scent on anyone else, but on Eli it was just perfect.

"I'll keep you safe," he murmured - and she believed it.

————————————

For the last few days life had settled back into something that *almost* resembled normalcy. Leah woke up, dropped Elizabeth off at her grandmother's before school, opened the bakery - and that was where she stayed until it was time to pick Elizabeth up from school. With the routine back in place she *almost* believed everything was fine.

That Thursday Leah woke up late. As she groggily threw on the first dress she grabbed from the wardrobe - a plain, dark green dress that hit her ankles, followed by a navy cardigan - she barely registered that Elizabeth was already pottering about downstairs.

Until a piercing *shriek* rang out through the house, echoing up the stairs and stabbing her right in the chest. With a gasp Leah flew downstairs, skirts billowing, and raced into the hall-

Elizabeth stood, wide eyed, at the open door. Her tiny hands clutched at her dress, lower lip pouting as if she was about to cry.

Leah swept her up into a tight hug, scooping her up to settle her on the lowest stair. "What happened?" she prodded gently - perhaps *too* gentle, but she had a terrible scare and didn't need to feel as if she was being interrogated.

Elizabeth sniffed, lip wobbling. "T-there's something on the porch. I think it's a rabbit." Big blue eyes gazed up at Leah, a silent plea to make everything okay; but Leah *couldn't*. They both knew that, really.

Instead, Leah simply pressed a kiss to her forehead and murmured, "let me have a look outside, okay?"

Honestly, Leah didn't know what to expect. Roadkill, perhaps - for although the neighbourhood wasn't particularly busy there were a few large that passed through daily. What she *saw* was a dead rabbit, yes - but it had been placed on the lowest step intentionally. Blood still dried on the hard wood, shining and damp in the morning sun. Beside it sat a letter, tucked underneath one paw to keep it from flying away in the breeze.

Leah didn't need to read that letter to know what it was.

"Is it dead?"

Leah spun too fast, bare feet stumbling, and ushered Elizabeth back inside. "Don't look at it honey," she requested quietly, "I'm going to call Eli, okay?"

"The Sheriff?"

"Uh huh." She let the door close behind her - and wasted no time in locking it once again. She chased Elizabeth upstairs first with a promise of an extra tasty breakfast and *maybe* a day off school if she did as she was told. Then she had the phone pressed to her ear as she cast a nervous glance to Elizabeth's retreating body.

This time, Eli knew it was her. "What happened?"

"Another letter," she answered with a heavy sigh, "and a dead rabbit."

"Dammit," Eli cussed - and although Leah didn't approve of such language she had to agree, if only in her mind. "Listen, I'm glad you called - I was just about to call *you.* We know who' been harassing you."

Her stomach jittered, heart skipped. Swallowing, the words caught in her throat as she asked, "who?"

"Murphy Chapman. He was a suspect for the last string of murders - remember I told you? - but he disappeared off the map around the time the murders stopped."

"And now he's back?" Leah concluded. Despite having only woken up ten minutes ago she was *exhausted,* and it took every ounce of energy to stay on her feet. "So you can arrest him?"

A sigh, followed by thick silence. Leah fidgeted, desperate to ask but knowing she had to give him time to think. Eventually he sighed for a second time, and she pictured him running a hand through his thick, dark hair. "It isn't that easy. He has no address and we haven't been able to track him down - he's damn good at hiding, apparently."

"I don't understand," Leah confessed after a moment, "he's killed so many people but he turned up to my house with nothing but a *knife*."

"I doubt he expected you to be armed," Eli explained, "the other women and kids were all suffocated in their sleep. Nasty way to go." He heaved one more sigh, muffled by the poor phone connection. "His own ex-wife and kid died five years ago in a break in gone wrong. The leading theory is... well, that he thinks by killing other mothers and their children he can somehow bring *his* back."

Silence. Thick, tense silence. Leah's heart skipped in her chest and she wanted to be *sick* - but what would that solve? Swallowing down the urge, she closed her eyes. "At least you know who it is," she replied quietly.

"I don't think it's safe for you at home," Eli put voice to her own thoughts. He sounded tense, nervous - and it was so unlike him that it alone made her pulse quicken. "I don't want you to take this the wrong way, Leah, but would you consider staying with me until this is all resolved?"

She couldn't help the little gasp of surprise that left her lips - and she was thankful that he couldn't see the dark flush that overtook her otherwise fair face. "I couldn't, really! You already have so much to deal with-"

"And I'd feel a lot better knowing you and Elizabeth are safe."

Biting down on her lip, Leah only sighed. "All right, if you're sure it isn't a bother," she finally conceded.

"You're *never* a bother, Leah," Eli murmured fondly, "I'll pick you up - pack anything you need and I can always stop by again for anything you forget."

Leah could have *kissed him* - he was just so endlessly sweet and considerate, not to mention handsome. In fact, as Leah hung up and called to Elizabeth, she realised the only thing stopping her from kissing him was her own timidness.

———————————

Sleep didn't come easily that night. Tucked away in Eli's spare bedroom with Elizabeth curled up by her side, Leah lay awake, staring at the dark ceiling, for two hours.

Finally, legs restless and mind wide awake, Leah shuffled out from beneath the safe haven of thick blankets - pressing a soft kiss to the sleeping Elizabeth in the process - and padded downstairs. Perhaps, after a drink of water and a quick check around the house - just to confirm everything was *fine* - she would eventually be able to sleep.

What she didn't expect was to see a light on in the kitchen, the door half closed. Sluggish footsteps pattered against the wooden floor, and she caught a quick glimpse of Eli, still fully dressed, as he passed by the gap of the half open door.

Leah hovered, a flush darkening her cheeks as she realised while Eli was dressed in dark jeans and a shirt, she wore only her nightgown and a thick, fluffy robe. It covered her from neck to ankles, the fabric thick to fight off the autumn chill, but she still tugged at the fluffy fabric as if to cover herself more decently.

"Leah?"

The soft call jolted her back to reality and she flushed *scarlet,* eyes snapping up to lock onto Eli's soft hazel ones. "Hi," she replied lamely.

"Couldn't sleep?" he questioned kindly, "me neither. Do you, uh, want a drink? I'm making tea." If Leah hadn't known better she would have thought his gaze lingered across her for just a moment too long, gaze dipping to her barely exposed collarbones beneath the robe. Then his eyes darted up to hers and he smiled, stepping aside so she could squeeze into the tiny kitchen.

As the Sheriff, Eli could have afforded a much larger house than the tiny cottage he lived in - but it had been his aunt's, and without any children of her own to leave it to, Eli was the lucky man she left it to in her will. She surmised he didn't have the heart to move. Besides it was cute, in a quaint and cramped sort of way - the kitchen was barely big enough for the dining table crammed against one wall, but it faced a beautiful backdrop of hills and mountains from the elegant window facing west. Leah understood why he loved this house.

A small part of her didn't want to leave.

Eli busied himself with mugs and tea, abandoning that venture half way through to rummage in the fridge for milk. "Just milk, right? You've never had much of a sweet tooth."

"That's right," Leah replied with a smile. It was sweet that he remembered something so simple as how she liked her drinks, even after so long. She remembered *his* preferences too - lots of milk and one spoonful of sugar - but that was besides the point. Settling onto the nearest chair, she regarded him through sleepy, lidded eyes.

When he placed a steaming mug of milky tea by her side, she gave him a thankful smile. Steam bloomed up and momentarily blocked her view, and she all but sank into the warmth it provided.

"So, what's on your mind?"

Leah blinked, lips parted even though no words came through. What *wasn't* on her mind? That was a better question. "I don't know," she admitted with a shrug. Small hands clamped around the hot mug. "It's just *everything.* A burglary I could have handled - but this is a real threat and I... I'm scared." Leah shivered, head ducked in embarrassment.

"You've every right to be," Eli assured. Just like last time, as their hands coiled together, Leah found herself flushing - but did she ever do anything else around him nowadays? His grip around her thin fingers were firm, warm and reassuring in a way only *he* achieved. It felt *right* despite the fatigue clogging her mind.

Smiling groggily, Leah took a sip of tea with her free hand. Even then, her eyes lingered on him. "You've done so much for me," she whispered, "a lot more than any Sheriff *has* to do. You're honestly a Godsend." The mug splashed tea from the rim as she set it down, but neither of them noticed as she reached out to sandwich her hands around his. Once again she was taken with just how *warm* he was, how gentle despite being such an enormous man.

His next words sent warmth spreading through her chest. "I'm not doing this as the Sheriff," he murmured, "but as your *friend.*" Even in the dimness of the late-night kitchen, Leah couldn't miss how he flushed. It made the dusting of freckles darker, standing out against his pink tinged skin.

Well, *that* was interesting. Perhaps it was her sleep fogged mind that made her brave, or perhaps it was how *gorgeous* Eli looked, dark eyes lidded with sleep and that goofy smile spreading across his lips. She felt herself leaning forward, even as the haze of her brain prevented her from *truly* realising where this was going.

At the same time, Eli's gentle hand detached from hers - only to curl against the base of her neck. Leah's heartbeat skipped and she let out a nervous giggle. Was this *actually* happening? Or was she really asleep in Eli's spare room, dreaming up this ridiculous, wonderful scenario?

When their lips met, soft and careful and almost *shy,* Leah knew without a doubt that it was real. He tasted of tea and cigarettes, and Leah almost missed the ever present coffee scent that always clung to him - that is, until his thick, sturdy arms wrapped around her torso and suddenly her mind went blank. Lost in the sensations of their warm bodies pressed together, everything else seemed to fade away.

Eli parted first, and Leah immediately missed his arms around her. "I'm sorry, was that too much?"

"Not at all," she assured - and then stifled a laugh behind one pale hand. It was so surreal as they sat there in the darkened kitchen, catching each other's nervous glances like lovesick schoolkids.

Frankly, Leah wouldn't have had it any other way.

"When this is all over," Eli suggested, "how about you and I go on a date?"

"I'd love to." And she *did,* so much that just the thought made her giddy, wide smile spreading across her full lips. If there had been any chance of her sleeping tonight she was *far* to awake now - just for a very different reason than before.

———————————————

Finally, Eli and Leah retired to bed, murmuring soft goodnights with sleepy kisses.

When Leah awoke it was to a cold, empty bed. For a moment she forgot where she was, blearily reaching for the clock on her side table even though it was still too dark to see. Then she remembered that she had been sharing the bed with Elizabeth - and bolted upright with a strangled gasp.

In less than a second she was on her feet, stumbling to the door. *It's fine,* her mind tried to reason, *she just got up for a drink or the bathroom.* Even as she bolted downstairs she knew it wasn't true.

And there he stood. Murphy Chapman, she presumed, was a tall man with broad shoulders and greasy black hair. Unlike last time he didn't bother to hide his face, pasty features on full view. But none of that mattered, not when he had her *daughter* held in his thick hands, fingers clinging to her shoulders so tightly that they left dark red marks.

"Let *go* of her," Leah blurted before she could stop herself. She stormed forward, eyes narrowed to slits - but then Murphy produced a knife from deep within his hoodie pocket and she froze.

"Don't move," he warned, "or she gets it."

Leah's eyes darted to Elizabeth. She was so small, tiny in his arms, and her round face was pale. Ashy. If it wasn't for the gasps that escaped her lips, Leah would have thought she was ready to pass out.

"Don't do this," Leah tried to reason, "she's *seven,* she hasn't done anything to you."

"Did you know," Murphy mused in the gravelly voice of a smoker, "you, Leah Bontrager, are the only widow in this neighbourhood? Maybe this entire town?"

Leah sucked in a breath. She had frightened him off once before - but back then she had a *rifle*. A useless one maybe, but only she had known. This time she had *nothing* - and he held a razor-edged knife to her daughter's throat. Swallowing, she tensed. "So?" she replied quietly.

"So, that made you an easy target. A young Amish woman raising a kid on her own, that's something you don't see often. I picked you out right away."

"For what?" she muttered. No matter how hard she tried, Leah simply couldn't look him in the eyes - they were hollow, not a man lost in grief like Eli had suggested but the dark, empty eyes of someone much, much worse.

The knife pressed into Elizabeth's delicate skin and she whimpered, cringing back even as Murphy held her tight. Leah lurched forward on instinct but Murphy dragged Elizabeth further into the hall. Their bodies were swallowed by the darkness. "Now, don't go trying anything."

The first time, he had been silent. Now he wanted to *talk* - and that was good. Leah's frazzled mind struggled, unable to form complete thoughts as she stared at the wide eyes of her child. But she had to *try*. Thinking about what Eli had told her, she asked, "why are you doing this? Do you think it will bring your family back?"

His lips curled, revealing yellow teeth to the dim lighting. "My *family* are none of your business."

"But you want them back? They were killed, weren't they?" She was rambling now, desperately trying to keep him talking, *distracted,* in the hopes Eli might appear. "You loved them."

Grey eyes narrowed in suspicion. "I did," he confirmed.

"Well I love my daughter, just like you loved yours. How does this *help,* killing children and mothers without regard for their lives."

It was the wrong thing to say. His white knuckle grip tightened around the knife and a thin dribble of blood dripped from Elizabeth's neck. Tears sprung to her eyes but she didn't make as sound as she twisted in his grasp. Murphy's other hand grabbed a fistful of hair and *yanked* her head back, holding her painfully in position. "If *you* die," he snarled, "then you can replace their position in the afterlife. I can have my *girls back.*"

He believed it with such conviction it left Leah speechless. Tears of her own sprung to her eyes, hands shaking. Someone like him couldn't be reasoned with - what would she say? He wouldn't believe her if she told him Heaven didn't work that way. In his mind, he had his own reality.

Yet he hadn't killed them yet. If he believed it, truly and without question, then Elizabeth and Leah would both be dead.

"Look," Leah began - and she stepped forward slowly, arms outstretched to show she meant no harm. Where she was taking this she didn't know, but it was working so far. "I know you loved them, and you miss them, but this hasn't worked so far. Why are we any different?"

"It has to work eventually," he muttered, eyes narrowed, "I just haven't found the right people yet. They-the circumstances have to match and you're the closest I've ever seen-"

The stairs creaked above them, painfully loud in the stillness of the house. Murphy's gaze whipped up and so did Leah's, eyes wide with relief. *Eli.*

"Get away from them." He raised a pistol, aimed right at Murphy's chest.

He did't budge. "This doesn't involve you-"

"I won't warn you again," Eli snarled - and it was so different to his usual, easy smile that Leah's heart skipped. "Lower the knife and move away."

He didn't. *Of course* he didn't. Murphy's lips peeled back as he pulled Elizabeth along the hall, spouting obscenities. The knife tightened in his grip as he held it to her throat - and then a gunshot resounded throughout the tiny house as Murphy crumpled, knife clattering to the ground.

Leah didn't pause to think, didn't pause to look at the man bleeding out onto the carpet. She ran to Elizabeth, wrapping her in warm arms and burying her face into Elizabeth's soft golden hair. "Are you all right, baby?"

She only squeaked in return, but wrapped her tiny arms around her mother, all but clambering into her lap.

Eli joined their side in an instant, muttering soft apologies as he bundled both Elizabeth and Leah into his massive arms. "It's over," he murmured into her ear, "you're both safe now."

"I almost got through to him," Leah sighed, "but it didn't work."

"You tried, that's what matters," Eli replied sincerely. He drew back and their eyes locked, a small smile gracing his lips.

Without thinking, Leah leaned across Elizabeth to press a soft kiss to his lips. "Thank you," she murmured, "you saved our lives."

"You saved yourselves," he replied as he kissed her again. He moved from her lips to her cheeks, then along her jaw - and despite it all Leah *laughed.*

"Are we going to be okay now?" Elizabeth questioned, voice tiny.

"Yes we are," Leah replied - and it was *true.*

AMISH VALLEY

MICHELLE BENTON

<u>January</u>

You have to stop this! Naomi chided herself, trying to silence what was happening in her head. But she could not stop her foot from tapping and her neck from bopping as she hummed under her breath. *Someone is going to catch you one day and then you'll have some explaining to do.*

She kept her head down so she would not be heard laughing. However, her snickers did not fall on deaf ears and when she turned her head from the firewood she was splitting, two of the women glared at her from their various vegetables.

"Do you find something amusing, Naomi?" Anke Hilty asked coldly but Naomi quickly shook her head and averted her eyes. Still, she could not stop the smile from toying on her generous mouth. She had only been welcomed into the district four months earlier but it seemed that Naomi was still regarded as Englisch to several of the women in the community. Naomi was smart enough to realize that it had little to do with her personally and more to do with upsetting tradition but it did not ease her sense of discomfort. Women like Anke and Anke's sister, Emma made the conversion to the Amish way of life difficult sometimes. If not for Naomi's unstoppable sense of humor, she was sure she would have returned to life in Indianapolis long ago. *I'll be an outsider until I get baptized,* she reasoned, turning her attention fully toward the garden now and forcing any other "English" thought from her head...like the popular song which had been playing over and over in her mind since she had woken at dawn.

"Naomi, you can't be serious!" her mother had screamed when Naomi had told of her plans to convert. "You can't go a day without the internet!"

Naomi had shaken her head, expecting the histrionics from her mother, inwardly relieved to know she would not have to listen to the woman's incessant shrieking day in and day out.

"I can and I will."

"We won't be able to visit you!" her father had protested. "They don't allow for outsiders in their community."

"I know! Isn't it wonderful?" As Naomi spoke, she genuinely meant the words. The Amish way of life, their seclusion, their devotion to each other and God was inspirational to her in every conceivable way.

But it had been Stephen who had almost made her change her mind.

"You can't run away from your problems by disappearing, sis," he told her. "You will just find yourself walking into a whole new whack of problems. But if this is what you want to do, I support you, no matter what. I hope you know I'll miss you."

His words had hit a sour note with Naomi and that night and every night subsequently, what he had said had rung in her head. *I am not running away,* she told herself over and over. *I am trying to under-complicate my very overcomplicated life. It is too messy now, filled with things I do not require. All I need is to surround myself with fresh air, hard work and true, unpretentious, like minded people.* She knew that her family was concerned about her mental state. Ever since her fiancé, Carlos had fled town with her best friend, things had begun to spiral downhill for Naomi. In the aftermath of the betrayal, she had set fire to all his belongings during an onset of uncontrollable fury. She had done so on the front lawn of the house they shared, hoping that Carlos would return and see a pile of ash where his beloved Gucci ties had once been. Carlos had never shown his face at the house again and unfortunately, the act had resulted in an arrest as the flame had spread, damaging the neighbor's car. She had been lucky, let off on probation as it was a first offense and then promptly fired from her job as a personal support worker.

"I'm sorry, Arry, I really am," her boss had told her, regret gleaming in his eyes. "But you can't have an arson record and work with the public, especially not in the medical field."

"I've been working here for four years! It was a stupid act of passion!" Naomi had protested, tears threatening to flow down her round cheeks as her full mouth quivered. "I am no danger to anyone!"

"I know that, Arry and you know that but you know you are required to have a clean record. I can't keep you employed with this agency any more." As he led her away in full blown sobs, he emptily promised to give her an excellent reference but he knew just as well as she did that no one was ever going to hire her again as a PSW. A felony was a felony after all. From there, she had been evicted as she wallowed in depression, eating ice cream and watching Netflix twenty hours a day. Naomi had not a cent in savings and between asking her parents for money and living on the streets, Naomi opted for the latter. She went to stay with Stephen for a short time before having an epiphany one day at the farmer's market; she would join the Amish. At the start, even she had recognized how obscure an idea it was but it did not stop her from investigating. She began frequenting the market more often, discovering that it was almost unheard of for outsiders to convert. Naomi pushed the issue, finding only two people who would entertain her questions. One was a man named Camp Girod, a solemn faced farmer who answered her inquiries in as few words as possible but Naomi soon learned that was his way of speaking and not rudeness. The other was Emma Hilty, a girl who had promised to become a fruitful friendship but had somehow fallen short down the line. Both had seemed happy that she had shown so much interest in their faith and were eager to educate her to the best of their ability. One afternoon, Camp brought the bishop of their district to meet with Naomi to answer some things they did not know. Naomi had almost hugged the tall, shy man but immediately stopped herself. *You must behave like a proper Amish woman from here on in,* Naomi told herself. *No more city girl shenanigans.*

The bishop initially had not been convinced by Naomi but as time went on, he began to recognize her intentions as true and slowly, with

Camp and Emma whispering praise in his ear, he eventually began to take her seriously.

"It is often very difficult for an outsider to simply assimilate into our culture. We don't have the luxuries which your kind seem to deem necessity to function," the Bishop had warned. "More often than not, the English return to the life in which they have been reared."

"That won't happen with me, Bishop!" Naomi declared with conviction. "I will be one hundred and twenty-five percent committed to the community. You'll see!"

The elderly man had raised a bushy eyebrow, somewhat distastefully at Naomi's loud proclamation.

"Naomi, in our community, patience and peace are considered large attributes. The quick tempered and moody do not fare well in our lifestyle," Bishop Kurtz continued. "We are one with God's teaching and he teaches the virtues of the meek. Do you believe you can follow those teachings?"

Naomi nodded eagerly although inwardly she cringed at her own lie. In truth, she had little religious teachings and knew very little about the Bible. She vowed that she would read the scripture from start to finish. *I'll do it in one sitting if that's what it takes!* In the end, Bishop Kurtz decided that Naomi would try the Amish way, largely influenced by Camp and Emma's convincing but partially enthralled by her belief that she was meant to be Amish. Under normal circumstances, the Bishop would not have entertained such an inane idea but Naomi had become a legend in the district and he had finally allowed his curiosity to get the best of him. Every evening after market, one of the parishioners would regale the bishop of tales. A young, bubbly woman would stop by their stalls at the market, begging for information about their culture. Most dismissed her, believing her to be a reporter and not wishing to fraternize with outsiders or disclose anything inappropriate. However, Emma had been amused by her tenacity and began to converse with the girl. She had been pleasantly surprised to discover that Naomi had a genuine desire to forsake the outside world and start fresh within the security of their community. Before long, Camp Girod, whose dairy booth neighbored Emma's meat display, heard the outgoing Naomi and found himself drawn into conversations also. If Emma and Camp had not been such upstanding members of the district, Bishop Kurtz would have never met Naomi Pryce. In the end, however, he was just as smitten with the girl as the other two members of his parish.

On a warm night in September, Naomi, in only a very simple skirt and white blouse, said good bye to Indianapolis and moved into the Hilty's home in rural Indiana with Bishop Kurtz's blessing.

That had been four months earlier. In that time, Emma had lost her good nature with Naomi. Naomi suspected it had much to do with the fact that Anke did not like her. Naomi tried to tell herself it did not matter, that she belonged there just as much as they did. *Just because I wasn't born into this life, doesn't make me any less Amish!* She pep talked herself. At that moment, another popular song blasted into her head. She shook her head mournfully. *My own psyche is mocking me.*

"It's raining on your head, Naomi and yet you seem so content, sitting there in the mud." Naomi whipped her head up and looked at the speaker. Anke and Emma's brother Evan stood above her, his light blue eyes twinkling with laughter. To her surprise, she realized he was right. The sunlight had disappeared and dark rain clouds had overtaken the sky. She suddenly realized that the Hilty sisters had retreated inside without saying a word. Water was seeping into her boots and the air had taken on a sudden chill. She rubbed her hands against her

"Come inside before you fall ill," Evan laughed, offering a hand. She eagerly accepted and followed the oldest Hilty sibling inside the farmhouse. Anke scowled at them from the window and Naomi realized she was still holding Evan's hand. Embarrassed, she pulled her palm from his and he turned, winking at her. Naomi blushed crimson. Evan had bestowed endless attention upon her since her arrival in the district. From the first night, he had told her stories on the porch and introduced her around to the neighbors. In turn, he asked that she tell him about the city, the sights and people. Naomi did her best to make it sound exciting, despite her recollection being less than glamorous but it seemed the more she embellished, the more captivated Evan became. Naomi had almost felt like he had claimed her but of course that was ridiculous. That was something the English would do, not the gentle-minded Amish. Still, Naomi was flattered and relished the friendship she found in Evan.

"Let me make some tea. You should change your clothes. I don't understand how you can be so at peace in the rain," Evan told her. "Especially someone so accustom to having warmth at their fingertips!"

Naomi shrugged. It was difficult not to be at peace in such surroundings. There was no bustle, no stress. The days were long, yes, but Naomi felt as if she had always been tilling fields and saying prayers. She hadn't been certain that the religious aspect would appeal to her, being reared nearly agnostic but the more time she had spent in worship, hearing God's plans, the more Naomi recognized what she had been missing from her life. *You made the right choice coming here,* she told herself as she quickly changed and brushed out her dark hair. She regarded her reflection in the mirror. She was an attractive woman by any standards; shoulder length straight brown hair, her bangs finally growing out from the blunt cut she had worn from before joining the community. Her dark eyes were intelligent and wide, her mouth constantly curved to a smile. Her inner happiness radiated outwardly and she found herself smiling in the glass.

"Are you coming?" Evan bellowed from downstairs. "The tea is becoming cold!"

"Yes!" Naomi yelled back and winced. *You need to tone it down!*

She hurried out of her small room and down the stairs to meet with Evan in the kitchen. Emma stopped her, stepping out from the shadows in the sitting room.

"Naomi," she said in a low voice. Naomi paused in surprise, glancing toward the kitchen but Evan was not standing there.

"You need to stay away from my brother," she warned. "Don't say I didn't warn you." Naomi felt her heart skip a beat. In the darkness of the hall, Naomi thought she saw a glint of anger in the younger girl's eyes. She did not reply, instead backing away, looking hurt at Emma's words, watching the younger girl disappear up the stairs. *I suppose I am not good enough for her brother, then? Am I always going to be an outsider? Will they never accept me here?*

"Naomi, would you care to take a walk with me after supper tomorrow?" Camp asked conversationally after worship. Naomi nodded.

"Of course," she replied, unsuspectingly. "I would love to!"

"There is a matter I would like to discuss with you," he said in his usual somber tone. Naomi smiled to herself but nodded again. She could not imagine Camp being anything but serious. *He probably wants to discuss the winter frost and he makes it sound like the world is about to come to an end,* she thought jokingly. She dared not jest with Camp. He was far too routine for such play. Naomi had once been present when Camp had been unwell and overslept as a result. She had never seen anyone so flustered in all her life. His entire demeanor had been altered and he snapped viciously at everyone in his wake. Naomi had been wounded by his sharp tones until Emma had told her that Camp was the most structured person in their district. From the time he was a child, he had risen with the roosters and planned every single minute of every day down to the second. When his schedule was disrupted, it made him confused and disoriented. After learning that, Naomi had gone out of her way to accommodate his whims. After all, if it had not been for Camp, she likely would never have been allowed in the community. Naomi owed him a debt of gratitude. Also, Camp was one of her only friends. She didn't know why, but Camp seemed to like her.

"You're not like anyone I would ever imagine Camp Giron associating," Anke told Naomi icily one day after Camp walked away. Naomi and he had been speaking over the fence for almost half an hour. Naomi had raised an eyebrow, stung by the connotation.

"And why not?" she demanded. "I am just as God fearing and hard working as anyone here, Anke! I wish you wouldn't imply that I'm not!"

"Maybe so," the older sister had replied. "But you are also the loudest. Camp is a quiet, gentle man. You are so...brash."

"Brash? I am not brash!" Naomi had yelled. Anke had smiled thinly as if to say "I rest my case." Naomi had gone out of her way to avoid speaking with Anke after that but Anke made it easy. She barely had two words to say to Naomi under the best of circumstances. Inwardly, though, she wondered what Camp found interesting about her. *Anke is not wrong. I am exactly the opposite of the man. I always thought that introverts found extroverts exhausting.* Naomi did not have to wait long to find out.

The following evening, the night had turned bitterly cold but after supper, Camp knocked on the Hilty door. Naomi hurried threw on her coat, scarf and gloves before adjusting her bonnet and heading toward the front door to meet her friend. Evan grabbed her by the arm as she went to leave the kitchen, a scowl darkening his fair face.

"Are you going out walking with Camp Giron?" he demanded. Surprised, Naomi nodded at the question.

"Yes," she answered, cocking her head in confusion. Evan's blue eyes narrowed dangerously.

"Is that a problem?" Naomi asked nervously. She studied his face for an answer and suddenly he realized how tightly he was holding her. Abruptly, he let her go, shame flooding his face.

"No, of course not," he told her hastily. "I – it's very cold outside is all. Please dress well." With that he disappeared into the back of the house, leaving Naomi staring after him, open mouthed. *Am I delusional or was that an act of jealousy?* She asked herself, a warm glow of happiness filling her insides. She had suspected that Evan liked her but he had never been anything more than friendly toward her even though the community called his ways flirty. She secretly hoped that he was jealous of Camp. She pushed Evan out of her mind as she remembered that Camp was waiting for her. *You must not make Camp wait,* she thought guiltily but Camp did not look perturbed as he stood in the foyer, chatting with Mrs. Hilty.

"Ah, there you are, Naomi. Please do not be late. We have a very busy morning tomorrow," the matriarch ordered and Naomi nodded obligingly. Naomi had never given the Hilty's any cause for alarm. She had done everything per her agreement with Bishop Kurtz.

"Remember, Naomi," Bishop Kurtz had told her when she had arrived. "It is not what I expect of you but what God and this community expect of you. You will see a reflection of yourself in every action, good or bad. The choice is yours but in the end, it is only you who must answer to God."

"Shall we?" Camp extended his arm and Naomi took it, smiling. The pathway to the road was icy and Camp held fast to her as she almost slipped several times.

"My goodness, Camp," Naomi exclaimed as ten minutes had only seen them a few hundred feet down the road. "Perhaps we should plan our walk for another night."

"I would prefer not to, Naomi if you do not mind indulging me." Naomi smiled and shrugged tolerantly. She could barely feel her face or toes in the extreme cold but she did not want to disappoint Camp.

"This sounds urgent, Camp. Of course, we can speak tonight. What is going on?"

Camp paused and looked down at her, his own dark eyes soulfully deep. He seemed to be thinking about his words and in spite of her resolve to be patient, Naomi wished he would spit it out. She flexed her fingers inside her gloves to ensure they were still there.

"Naomi, I am very proud of the way you have situated yourself in the community," he began. She smiled, abashed by the praise.

"I couldn't have done it without you, Camp. You know that, right?"

"I believe that your perseverance would have paid off regardless of my small role. However, I am happy you are here."

"I am thrilled to be here!" she announced. He nodded soberly and cocked his head.

"Have you given any thought to your baptism?" he questioned.

"Bishop Kurtz has suggested April. Personally, I would like to do it tomorrow but I confess, I never much wanted to join the Polar Bear Club." A look of confusion passed over Camp's eyes and Naomi realized he didn't understand the reference. *You really need to get your head out of the English,* she scolded herself again.

"Anyway, you'll know when I know. I'm pretty sure everyone around here gets an invite, right? Is that what you want to talk about? You're worried I might go back to the city after everything you've done to bring me here?" she asked, smiling. Camp's brow furrowed and Naomi realized that he had not entertained that thought whatsoever, at least not until she had brought it up.

"No..." he said slowly. "That was not what I wanted to speak to you regarding."

He said nothing and Naomi felt a smidgen of annoyance. *I know patience is a virtue but I'm becoming an ice sculpture here!*

"Camp, you're my friend, you know that, right?" He nodded, seemingly more confused by the conversation shift.

"As my friend, probably my best friend here, I am begging you to ask me whatever it is because I am freezing to death! I swear there are corpses warmer than me right now!"

Camp inhaled sharply and nodded.

"I wanted to ask you, if, once you get baptized..."

"Yes?"

"If you would consider giving me your hand in marriage?"

<u>**April**</u>

"Welcome, Naomi Pryce to our community!"

A cheer erupted and Naomi, soaked to her knickers, beamed at the crowd which surrounded her. She noted with pride that even Anke nodded in approval, a thin, funny smile pursing her lips. *I am one of them now! Finally! They can't call me an outsider anymore!* She thought. She turned to Bishop Kurtz and bowed slightly in thanks.

"We are pleased to have you, Naomi. You have demonstrated the loyalty, hard work and patience which we value so highly. If only you would work on your Pennsylvania Dutch..." A small chuckle flew through the group and Evan lunged forward to take her arm.

"Everyone speaks English anyway, *liebchen*. Come on, Arry. Let's eat!" Happily, she allowed herself to be led toward the Hilty barn where a feast had been set up for the baptism. Out of the corner of her eye, she saw Camp standing alone, under a tree, looking forlorn.

Since the frigid night of their walk, Camp had not come calling and Naomi admitted that she missed his company terribly. Of course, Evan was her constant companion, joking and laughing with her, despite the tongue wagging of the community.

"She does not behave properly," some of the older women complained. "She flirts recklessly with the Hilty boy and she lives in that house!"

"He is no better," others countered. "He has been brought up right in this community and he blatantly disregards our traditions. He acts like he has English blood."

But neither Evan or Naomi seemed to mind the gossip. It was not because they did not hear of it; in fact, Mr. and Mrs. Hilty often forbade them to be together alone but they still managed to find a way to see one another and enjoy each other's company. Naomi had been counting the days to her christening. She knew that the moment she officially became Amish, Evan would ask her to marry. *I wonder if he will do it today even,* Naomi thought, peering at him out of the corner of her eye. He returned her look of adoration and impulsively squeezed her hand, not releasing it. Naomi did not take her palm away this time, despite the looks she received from the members. She could almost hear their thoughts; *she just got accepted into the fold and look at her! Acting like a fallen woman!* Naomi did not care. She was incredibly happy and she knew she was about to become happier.

The day progressed beautifully. There was food and banter. The only dark cloud was Camp's almost palpable sadness. She had not outright refused his pre-emptive proposal but she had let him down in a way that he knew she did not see a future with him. *Camp will find someone. He is dependable and hardworking. Any woman in the community would be lucky to have him.* But the thoughts did not alleviate Naomi's guilt and she forced herself to focus on the festivities. As the afternoon wound into evening, she found herself exhausted. The events of the day had taken a toll on her and she wanted to retire early for the evening. She excused herself just after dark and retreated to her bedroom. As she lay in bed, a smile touching her lips, she knew that tomorrow would be the day Evan would ask her to marry him.

"Naomi!" She bolted up in her bed, scared out of a dream state. It took her a moment to reconcile her surroundings and then, through the dark, she peered at Emma and Anke who stood in the doorway, both relief and anger written on their faces.

"What?" she croaked, her throat like cotton. "What happened?"

Emma exhaled slowly and crept into the dark room, clutching a letter in her hand.

"You're still here."

"Well I almost jumped out of my skin but yes, I am still here. What is going on?" Naomi demanded, throwing her legs over the side of the twin bed and rubbing her eyes.

"We thought you had gone with him," Anke answered crisply, also entering the room. She snatched the paper out of Emma's hand and flung it at Naomi.

"Gone with who? Guys, it's a little early in the morning for brain teasers. Can you tell me what is happening or can I go back to bed?"

"Do you know anything about this?"

Naomi picked up the single sheet of paper and read the note scrawled on the blank canvas.

Dear *Daed, Mammi,* Anke and Emma,

You have always done your best for me but I have never felt like I belonged in this community. I think I always knew that I would leave at some point but it wasn't until Naomi came that I knew the world was calling me. I could not stop thinking about the places she told me, the foods she had eaten, the people she met. I could not understand why she would give that all up to live here, in this boring, judgemental place. I have gone to the city. Don't worry about me, please. I am sure I will make my way just fine. I know this comes as a disappointment but I could not bear the thought of spending my life farming. I love you all.

Yours Always,

Evan

P.S. Tell Naomi if she changes her mind to come and find me in Indianapolis.

Slowly, Naomi read and reread the letter until tears began to slip down her cheeks and blot the ink on the paper. Anke grabbed it and swatted the water from the page scowling.

"*Mamm* and *Daed* haven't read it yet, Naomi. Don't ruin it. You've already ruined enough around here." Anke spun on her heel and stormed out the door, leaving Emma behind. The younger sister looked at Naomi's devastated face and gently placed her hand upon her shoulder.

"I told you to stay away from Evan," she murmured. "Not because you're not good enough for him but because he is not good enough for you."

<u>May</u>

"Naomi, you have been moping around here for a month now. I miss your sunny smile," Bishop Kurtz told her one day as he passed by the farm.

"I am not moping, Bishop!" Naomi protested. "I am working!"

"Yes, yes you are working and doing a fine job, I might add," he agreed. "But you need to forget about Evan. I understand you were very fond of him."

"He was my friend." Naomi dropped the hoe and stared at the bishop. The look was enough to stop him from uttering his next thoughts but his eyes travelled over her head to look at something in the distance.

"Well, I still miss your smile, child," he told her. "And sometimes when God closes a door, he opens up a window." She followed his gaze as he turned to leave and she saw Camp approaching in a wagon.

"Good day, Naomi," Camp greeted, somewhat nervously. "Would you care to go for a ride? I have an appointment with a medical doctor in town today."

Immediately, Naomi was concerned.

"Are you all right?" she asked, hurrying forward, wiping her dirty hands on her apron.

"Oh yes. Nothing serious. But I wouldn't mind the company," he replied. Naomi nodded quickly. *It is serious enough for him to ask her for companionship after an estrangement*, she thought nervously.

"Just give me a minute to change."

She was beside him in the carriage in minutes and they rode silently for a while.

"Naomi, when are you going to stop brooding about?"

"I am not brooding!" she snapped. *I'm not brooding! I am pining. Evan could come back any day. That is not brooding or moping. That is called being hopeful.*

"Fine." They continued their trip quietly. Naomi realized how unfair she was being to Camp. Camp was there. Evan was not. Camp stood by her. Evan hadn't even asked if she wanted to go with him. Why would she not give Camp a chance?

"I'm sorry, Camp," she finally said. He shot her a look out of the corner of his eye.

"What for?"

"I don't deserve your affections. You have been too good to me since the beginning."

"You are very worthy of all things good, Naomi. It has been my pleasure you call you my friend."

Naomi looked at him, his noble face proud and unsmiling.

"Would it be your pleasure to call me your wife?"

October

When their engagement was announced at worship, Naomi was met with genuine adulation.

"Camp Giron is a fine man. He will be Bishop one day, I promise you. You have made the right decision," Bishop Kurtz told her. "And I do believe you have made the man very happy. I have known Camp since he was a boy. I could count the amount of times he has smiled on one hand since then. Until you came along, Naomi. He adores you."

"He is a wonderful man," Naomi agreed, shooting her fiancé a look from across the salon. He met her gaze and smiled. Bishop Kurtz opened his mouth to say something else but seemed to reconsider.

"I hope you two will be very happy together, Naomi."

"I hope so too," she replied, a sudden stab of sadness overwhelming her. She would be lying to herself to say she didn't still think of Evan. She wondered if he was faring well in the city and if he ever thought about her. She knew that he wasn't coming back.

"He would not be welcome here if he did," Anke spat when Naomi asked her about him one night. Naomi had been shocked at the venom attached to his sister's words. Later, Emma pulled her aside.

"I know you were rather fond of my brother," Emma told her. "But there are many things you did not know about him."

Naomi arched an eyebrow. She wasn't sure she wanted to hear anything negative about Evan but curiosity got the better of her.

"Such as?" But Emma pursed her lips together as if she had already said too much.

"Just believe me, Naomi. You are marrying a good man in Camp. He will always do right by you." The words meant little to Naomi who lay awake at night, listening for sounds, dreaming that Evan would sneak back into the house and into her life again.

<u>November</u>

"You are a lovely bride," Emma whispered, adjusting the wreath of flowers about Naomi's head. Naomi smiled genuinely and gave her a hug.

"I don't think I've ever thanked you for all you've done for me, Emma," she told the younger girl. The blonde blinked and looked confused.

"What have I done?"

"You have helped give me a sense of community and family, one I have never had. I know you don't think I belong here but I want you to know that I care more about these people and our way of life than anyone or anything I have before in my life."

"I know you belong here, Naomi. That is why I asked Bishop Kurtz to speak with you. Camp and I saw the purity in your soul from the first day we met you. You are exactly the kind of person we want walking among us." The women smiled at each other and for the first time since Evan had left, Naomi felt truly happy. *I do belong here. I am one of them. Thanks to Emma and Bishop Kurtz. And thanks to Camp.*

"Shall we?" Emma offered Naomi her arm and the two made their way into the church where Camp stood waiting at the altar. Naomi felt like she was seeing him for the first time. He looked so handsome, his dark hair shining under his hat, two glossy curls hanging about his chiseled features. His eyes were alight with adoration as he watched his bride to be slowly walk toward him. His face broke into a beam so broad, Naomi was sure his face would crack from the force. Tears misted his irises. Emma gently squeezed her arm and released toward Camp. Suddenly, an abrupt gust of wind flew through the small chapel, extinguishing several of the lamps. Bride and groom turned toward the entrance where a form stood, panting in the opened doorway.

"Evan!" Naomi gasped. Immediately, Mr. Hilty rose to his feet, his face crimson in anger.

"How dare you show your face in here!" he thundered.

"I am not here for you, *Daed*," Evan retorted, his eyes remaining on Naomi as he stumbled up the aisle.

"Naomi, don't marry him!" he called as he approached. "Come back to the city with me. I made a mistake leaving you here but you're all I can think about." A murmur flowed through the crowd. *He did think about me! He does miss me!* Naomi thought, dumbfounded. Evan was at the altar, grabbing for her hands, his blue eyes pleading.

"I'm sorry! I made a mistake," he said again, his mouth turning up into a smile of contrition. Naomi glanced up at Camp, who had lost the rare beam which had lit up the church. She looked at Emma who shook her head woefully and stared at her shoed. Her gaze shifted to Bishop Kurtz whose mouth had formed a fine line. She stared into the crowd and took in Evan's family's look of shame and fury. Then she looked back at Camp again.

"I'm sorry," she whispered at him and Camp hung his head in defeat, his shoulders visibly sagging. Evan tightened his grip on her hands and Naomi yanked them back, her eyes still trained on Camp.

"I am sorry," she said again, reaching up to wipe the tears falling onto his cheeks. "I am sorry that I ever made you hurt. I am so sorry that I wasted any time on this man. I am so terribly sorry that I ever doubted my future is in your arms. I love you, Camp." She turned furiously to Evan who had gone pale at Naomi's speech.

"But Naomi – "

"What kind of disgusting man claims to love a woman and leaves her for months only to barge in on her wedding? You're despicable, Evan. And you're not welcome in our community – my community! Get out and don't return." After a stunned second of silence, Evan whirled on his heel and ran out the door.

"And you don't even close the door behind you! Can you imagine marrying such a man?" Naomi yelled after him. Applause and laughter broke out and someone hurried to shut the double doors and relight the kerosene lamps. Naomi took Camp's hands in hers and they gazed into each other's eyes lovingly.

"Now, where were we?" she asked Bishop Kurtz without looking away.

END

AMISH AMITY

Chapter 1

Rain just kept falling, never ending without any intention to stop, large puddles had gathered on the muddy grounds around the big barn, and water gushed down the eroded embankment running alongside the road, causing the road to be completely flooded. But no amount of rain would prevent Amity, Betty and Rachel to do what they came here to do. Having been friends since childhood, the three women were inseparable. Neither of them were married or promised to anyone yet, and although they are well beyond the age most girls in their community starts to settle down to start a family, it never really bothered them.

Amity was strong willed and mouthy young woman, who voiced her opinion whenever she felt it mattered. Of course her father, Bishop Gunther didn't quite approve of her behaviour at times, but he did support her willingness to stand up for herself. Bishop Gunther on the other hand wasn't like most others in their faith; he was more lenient and accepting than most, always promoting change within reason. He insisted that households started using gas stoves instead of coal stoves. He had even arranged to buy a truck to help the community to cart goods to the local market in town. According to him, modern change to a bare minimum does not give the devil a foothold, it just shows the devil that they are capable of change without modern ways ruling their lives and changing who they are or distracting them from things that matter most.

Betty, much like Amity also had a strong personality, one she definitely got from her mother, but she also had a mischievous streak. When the elders instructed the children not to play in the rain, she was always the first to splash in muddy puddles. When they had their social events, she was the one who would pull pranks, like stuff a mouse in someone's pocket or stick a dish to a table cloth with workman's glue, causing a huge disaster when someone tries to pick it up. All innocent pranks at most, but that was how everyone knew her and more often than not, when she was younger her father would ground her for punishment, but she always found a way out of it.

And then there was Rachel, shy quiet Rachel. More like the runt of the litter, she was one of few words and always just tagged along because Amity and Betty insisted. Rachel only had a father; her mother died giving birth to her. Her father eventually married Elsa, a widow with two sons, who she never got on with. They were two brats and she ended up spending more time with her friends than her own family and over the years, the trio had become the best of friends

Betty giggled and Amity squirmed on the bale of hay, "I bet you David looks like that when he takes his shirt off," she said pointing to the male model in the fashion magazine.

Amity giggled, "It's scandalous! If your dad knew you had these, he'll shun us all," she said in jest.

Rachel, curious as ever, was sitting on the left, also peeking at the magazine, one of the few they kept hidden in the barn under one of the wooden floor slats. They always snuck to the barn to page through the magazines and weigh every other man in their town up against the likes of models that posed so shamelessly with nothing but pair of underpants on.

"Jah! Well he doesn't know now does he?" Betty said and paged through a few more pages.

Rachel would never admit it out rightly but she also felt a slight tingle of excitement when she looked at these magazines, they were not overly crude, but they showed more flesh than she had ever seen in her life. Maybe it was because of this, that they were all still single, she thought. Comparing the local boys to those men were like comparing apples with onions.

A sudden noise quickly alerted them and Betty shoved the magazine behind the bale of hay they were seated on. Both Amity and Betty grabbed their egg baskets, while Rachel stood around looking as guilty as ever.

"Betty, are you girls here?"

It was Betty's father who called, and Rachel's stomach lurched, if the Bishop had any idea what they were up to they will be in so much trouble.

"We're here *daed*!" Betty called and dusted the hay off of her dress, "We were caught in the rain, and were waiting for it to pass," she said as her Bishop Gunther appeared.

"I thought so, well I have come to get you girls home, the storm is a long way from being over," he said and handed each of them a rain coat, "Better we hurry, or the storm will catch up with us," he urged them as he let each one of the girls walk towards the barn door ahead of him.

The sky was dark and it wasn't just a summer shower, it was a downpour that looked more like a waterfall from heaven. Heavy drops struck the ground tunnelling into the earth. Up ahead stood the buggy, which didn't offer much or any shelter and Rachel wasn't so sure if they would make it to their respective homes in one piece. Betty was the first to step into the rain, followed by Amity. Bishop Gunther looked at her and nodded, and then in a huddled group the four of them ran towards the buggy, careful not to slip and fall.

Thankful that there was still some daylight to guide the way, the three girls clung to each other as Betty's father steered the buggy towards the house. Hardly able to see a few feet ahead of them and on a treacherous road that has been washed away in most places, Bishop Gunther was still able to make them feel at ease. He didn't even look worried, but then again, that was probably how a man of God should be, like Paul walking on water.

The buggy wheels rattled as they rode over rocks and muddy trenches formed by the mass of water running diagonally across the small road. And a trip that normally took less than fifteen minutes to travel, now seemed like an eternity. They were slowly making their way ahead through the stormy downpour, unbeknownst to Bishop Gunther, the road up ahead had turned into complete sludge and the moment the buggy reached it, the wheels simply slid into a deep trench on the side of the road, pulling the buggy, with the horse off and on to the side of the road. The girls screamed in panic as the buggy slowly leaned over to its side, threatening to topple over. Rachel was the first to clobber out and then helped the other two on to the road. Betty got out safely, but as Amity stumbled out of the buggy, she stepped in a hole and twisted her ankle.

"Ow!!" she cried out as she fell to the ground grabbing for her ankle.

"Amity!" Betty cried and ducked down to help her friend, "Where does it hurt?"

Bishop Gunther also hunched down and looked at her ankle, "It's quite swollen, I think you may have sprained it, can you try and step on it?"

Betty and her father helped Amity to her feet, but the moment she put weight on her injury, she cried out in agony.

"We will have to get you home, just lean on me and Betty" the Bishop said. He studied the state of the buggy, "The buggy will have to stay here until morning."

"But papa, we can hardly see in front of us," Betty lamented as she supported her friend.

"The Lord will light our way," Rachel said confidently and gave Betty a gentle reassuring squeeze.

With Amity supported by Bishop Gunther and Betty, and Rachel next to them carrying the egg baskets, they started down the path taking carful steps in the dark.

Through the stormy gale and rain that kept showering, they heard a galloping sound that sounded more like thunder coming towards them and the next moment, a man on horseback arrived completely drenched.

Rachel couldn't make out his face, but right now he was the best thing that could have happened to them.

"Bishop, Maryanne sent me to see what was keeping you," he shouted over the raging storm, "What happened to the buggy?"

Rachel took over from the Bishop, while he explained to the stranger exactly what had happened, and suggested that they come to recover the buggy in the morning once the rain has passed.

"Betty, you will have to get on the horse with Amity, Rachel you will walk with Uri and I," the Bishop instructed and then the stranger named Uri, helped Amity, and then Betty on to the horse.

Together they slowly made their way back to society, the first stop was Amity's house, where the Bishop helped to get her inside, and seen to, then it was Rachel's turn and finally Uri, Bishop Gunther and Betty made their way to the Bishop's house.

~*~

After Rachel had changed into her night dress and towel dried her wet hair, she deposited herself in front of the fire place. The night had turned out a complete disaster. She was sure it was punishment for their bad behaviour. Lusting like that over fictitious men and so on. She wrapped her quilt around her shoulders and reached for her bible. She knew better than to let her judgement be influenced by anyone. Despite the guilt, she somehow found her mind drifting to the stranger who came to their aid. She still couldn't see his face clearly, but she was sure he was handsome, and strong.

She shook her head to chase away the thoughts and closed her eyes, and said a silent prayer of repentance. She was never going to look at those magazines again.

Chapter 2

The sun broke through the parted curtains in Rachel's room and she pinched her eyes shut. The night before had taken its toll on her, and resulted in her oversleeping when there was still so much to do. She was yet to feed the geese and get ready to go to the local market to deliver the eggs she had collected the day before, but she simply had no will power.

"Rachel!" Her step-mother called from the kitchen, "Come have your breakfast!"

Rachel covered her eyes with her forearm and sighed. She just needed a few more minutes of sleep, but she knew where her priorities lay. She willed herself out of bed and rushed around the room to get ready for the day. By the time she got to the kitchen her mother had already cleaned the dishes, and Rachel's breakfast was waiting.

"The Bishop and his friend were here earlier," Elsa commented in passing, "Looks like you girls had a rough night."

"Yeah, we got caught in the storm," she mumbled.

So the stranger is one of the Bishop's friends, which means he was old, she thought to herself.

"Apparently Amity had twisted her ankle quite badly, but she will be fine in a few days."

"I figured. She stepped in a hole when she tried to get out of the buggy, we couldn't see much."

Elsa came to sit at the table with her, "You girls need to be more careful, things could have been a lot worse."

Sometimes Rachel couldn't help but wonder what Elsa's agenda really was. At times she treated her like a stranger, barely paying attention to her, and other times she came across all motherly. And all this time Rachel had no choice but to keep her own emotions all bottled up.

"We will," Rachel said and stood up to wash her plate, "I'm taking the eggs to the market, is there anything you need me to do?"

"Oh not to worry about the eggs, I've already sold delivered them this morning."

Rachel felt as if she could crush the plate in her hands. Those eggs were her eggs, her income. She was saving money for herself, and now Elsa had taken the little bit she could earn for herself.

"Thank you," she said tight lipped without turning around.

"I hope you don't mind, your father does need some money to buy that new gas stove so, I figured every penny would help."

"Of course," Rachel turned around this time, with a fake smile plastered on her face, "I'll just get more eggs to get money for my new dress."

"Why on earth would you need a new dress?" Elsa said with mock surprise, "Don't you have enough as it is?"

Rachel was slowly starting to lose her temper, but she fought hard to remain calm, "I only have three dresses, and I need one for church, the others are all worn and faded."

Elsa laughed, "It's not like you'll be catching anyone's eye, and you're past the point of marriage. You're already considered a spinster."

"I'm only twenty-two, the same age my mother married," Rachel protested.

"And see how that turned out."

Elsa had barely said the words when her sons, Caleb and Alfred came into the kitchen, and Rachel had to hide her anger. She simply scooped up her empty egg baskets and stormed out of the house. How that woman dared say such heartless things and get away with it, was beyond her she thought as she marched determinedly in no particular direction. But as the anger subsided, it was replaced by doubt. Maybe it was too late for her to marry, but then the same applied to Betty and Amity, they were both the same age. Obviously living in Derby Creek wasn't much help either, there were far more women than men here, and unless they had gatherings from nearby towns, chances of finding a suitor was slim.

First of all there was Betty, who insisted that she was waiting for Mr Right, she refused to settle for less, then there's Amity who also had her own ideas of a suitor, and the few men that did ask for her hand in the past, were coldly turned down because she was just not interested. Rachel always thought that Amity was the kind who would go on a Rumspringa if her father allowed her, out of the three friends, she was the adventurous one.

Rachel grunted a loud oomph as she collided with someone sending her baskets flying. Thankfully they were empty; otherwise they would both have been covered in egg yolk. She stumbled back and started to apologize profusely when she swallowed her words, and a pair of very strong hands cupped her shoulders.

"Are you alight?" the young man asked, and offered her a lopsided smile.

"Jah, I am fine, I-I wasn't paying attention, I'm sorry," she said struggling to breathe.

"It's quite alright, you were miles away there for a second, I'm Uri, Rachel right?" he said and released her as he tucked his thumbs into his suspenders.

Uri, the name immediately rang a bell. He was Bishop Gunther's friend, but how? He was so young, she wondered.

"How do you know my name?" she asked foolishly.

"I came to your rescue last night in the storm, but I suppose you won't recognise me, it was rather dark."

"Oh! Oh right, yes. Well... um, I'll be going now. Thank you, I mean sorry, I... I have to go."

Rachel just about ran away from him, she had acted like a complete and utter fool, stuttering over her words like a second grader having to do an oral assignment. No wonder she was single. She couldn't sit in the company of a man without feeling awkward. As she hurried away she could feel his eyes burn into the back of her, but she refused to glance back. The farther she got away the quicker her out of control heart and raging butterflies would quieten down.

"Rachel!" It was Betty who waved her down, "Where are you heading?"

"Eggs!"

"You're going to Eggs?" Betty giggled.

"No, ugh, I'm going to collect eggs silly," she corrected herself as Betty fell into step next to her, "How is Amity doing?"

"She's fine, but you look like you've seen a ghost, why are you in such a hurry," Betty said as she tried to keep up to Rachel's pace.

"I need to sell enough eggs to buy a new dress. The cow sold all the eggs I collected yesterday."

"What a cow, did she not even ask you?"

"Does she ever?"

The rest of the way, the two friends walked in silence, Betty on her own planet, and Rachel trying to get Uri out of her mind. She hadn't expected him to be so young, nor did she expect him to know her name. The night before was a bit of a blur with everything going on, and she mostly remembered walking beside Bishop Gunther while Uri guided the horse by its reins with Amity and Betty on horseback.

"Is Uri your..."

"Don't you think Uri is..."

They both said at the same time and then burst out laughing.

"Uri is so handsome," Betty continued, "The last time I saw him was when we were kids. His family has been in Germany for the past few years."

"I didn't expect him to be so young," Rachel said, "Are they staying here?"

"Only Uri, he's staying at our house and is helping papa with a few things."

Rachel could hear by Betty's tone that she was keen on Uri, and she knew by the seam of her dress, that Amity will be just as taken by him.

One of them will most certainly catch his eyes, she thought and smiled softly. Her friends or at least one of them deserved a good strong man to care for them.

She dismissed the notion of Uri straight away, knowing that she would never stand a chance. She could hardly string together a proper sentence when she bumped into him earlier.

Chapter 3

Amity humped along with a crutch in one hand, while Betty excitedly skipped besides them. For the first time in who knows how long, Betty and Amity had made some effort to look presentable, both of them had brand new dresses. It was the Friday night frolic, where most boys got to voice their intentions.

Betty was nervous; as usual she was shy and nervous. She never liked these events much, she did not trust the thing called love, her father loved once, he had promised his mother that he would make sure she was taken care of, but now years later, all she had to remember her mother by was a single letter, and a lifetime of regret. Elsa was kind in some ways, but she was jealous of Betty, and Betty never did much right in her eyes.

The people from the surrounding farms started to arrive, old and young, in the middle of the big barn the table was set as always. Food in excess was spread across the table, along with lanterns casting a dim glow over everything.

"Have you seen how handsome Uri is?" Betty whispered under her breath.

Amity giggled and shifted in her chair, "I know right? I can still feel his hands on my hips as he helped me on to the horse."

"Oh and weren't they the biggest stronger hands ever?" Betty swooned.

"I'm going to make a play for him you know?" Amity murmured under her breath.

"No you're not, I am, and I've already spent some quality time with him."

Betty wagged her brows and reached for bunch of grapes.

"You can't eat now, we have to say thanks first," Amity said slapping Betty's hand.

"Oh please, no one is even looking."

Betty listened to her friends as they cooed over the newcomer and she opted not to show any interest. They had reason to try and win his affection, she had none. She will see this night through and make the best of a bad situation. Besides, she had a lot more on her mind. Maybe it was time she accepted the fact that she was a spinster, and she figured it was time she spoke to the Bishop and go his take on her moving out of her paternal home into her own. She could always offer her help as a teacher. She knew how to read, in fact she loved reading. She could go spend time at the local school and read to the youngsters, even help the school teachers to give extra lessons in literacy.

"Rachel!" Amity's voice broke into her thoughts.

"Oh... sorry I wasn't listening," she apologised.

"I was saying, maybe all three of us should play for Uri, we can see which one he picks."

Rachel raised her brows, "He's not up for auction, it's a silly game you're wanting to play."

"Stop being such a drab! It will be fun."

No it won't, she thought. The first thing that is bound to happen is that Uri will pick either Betty or Amity, then that will leave one or the other angry and disappointed, ruining a friendship of many years.

"I'm not a drab, I'm just saying. What if he picks Betty, then you'll be angry, not?"

Amity rolled her eyes, "You take things way too seriously, if he picks Betty, then so be it, I'm hardly desperate to marry."

"Come on Rachel, it will be fun; besides, maybe he shows no interest in any of us, then at least we know we all tried."

Betty worried her lip and looked down at her hands, "I don't know, I suppose no harm can come of it." She for one knew that she won't be the least bit phased if he picked Amity or Betty, because she knew she stood no chance.

Amity shoved her elbow into Rachel's ribs and gestured with her head towards the door. Talk of the devil, Uri was heading straight down the path on the opposite side of the table with his eyes fixed on them. And once again the sight of him made her heart race and as she watched him approach it was as if all else around her faded. She had tunnel vision and it was only him looking straight at her. When he finally stopped and took a seat directly opposite her she averted her eyes immediately. Of course, Amity kicked her under the table and Rachel cleared her throat uncomfortably.

"*Hallo* Uri," she said.

"*Hoe gaan het*, Rachel?" he smiled.

She only nodded, her tongue felt like led in her mouth, and her palms were sweaty.

Betty and Amity both fell right into conversation, putting their best foot forward while Rachel wanted nothing but to flee. Soon enough the evening got on the way, with youngsters all frolicking and enjoying the event. Uri made sure he mingled with everyone and never let on that he was interested in any of them in particular, which was funny, since Betty put her best foot forward and out rightly told him he had beautiful eyes.

As the evening drew to a close and most of the people had left, the last remaining few spent the rest of the time talking about the up and coming barn raising event. Uri was still seated across from Rachel, and Betty and Amity had moved closer to where Bishop Gunther was. He was playing the harmonica, which was probably the only instrument allowed in the community, but still sounded like heaven.

"So Rachel, have you always lived here?" Uri asked curiously as he picked on some of the bread sticks on his plate.

"*Jah*, I was born here," she said and offered him a shy smile.

"I'm surprised I don't remember you?"

"I'm not exactly the most memorable of all," she laughed.

"Oh but you are, you are a very beautiful woman."

Rachel blushed profusely and covered the side of her face with her hand, "Thank you," she mumbled.

"Can I pick you up for church on Sunday?"

Shocked at his request, Rachel shifted uncomfortably in her seat and worried her lip, as tempting as it was, she wasn't so sure if it was a good idea. But then again, Betty and Amity did say that they should all try and win his affection. She looked down at her empty plate and smiled. Perhaps it was time she stepped out of her comfort zone and tried dating at least, after all, he was simply going to take her to church, and it wasn't like he was proposing to her at all.

"Sure," she said and then got up, "I have to go now. I will see you around."

She saw his mouth open and close, but she rushed away regardless. She said her goodbyes to her friends and the rest of the community who were all still in the barn and headed home. Her mind was racing and her heart even more. For the life of her she couldn't understand what Uri saw in her. *You're a beautiful woman* – he had said, and it made her feel as if she was about to fly into the night sky on wings of angels. No boy, or man for that matter, had ever paid her such a compliment, and coming from someone as handsome and Uri, made her tummy do strange things.

Chapter 4

Uri was up and ready long before dawn on Sunday, making sure his buggy was clean and that he too was dressed in his best church clothes. He couldn't deny the fact that he felt bad for Betty, she had shown her affection so openly, but there was just no chemistry between them. Unlike Rachel, Betty was just too flamboyant to his liking. She was a pretty woman, but not even nearly as pretty as Rachel. Rachel was unusually pretty, with red hair that always seemed so perfectly plated and rolled up under her prayer cap, with loose strands that tickled her cheeks. The slight dusting of freckles across her nose, that spread to her cheeks made her even prettier, almost innocent not to mention the way she blushed every time he spoke to her.

He was quite surprised when she accepted his request to start off with, but pleased nonetheless.

The first night he saw the shy girl, with her baskets filled with eggs, he was intrigued. She was in control despite the stormy weather and their predicament, and even when he lifted the other two on to the horse, she never uttered as single complaint. She walked quietly next to them as if she was taking a stroll. Not even the rain slanting heavily against them broke through her composure. Maybe it was the way she kept to herself, or the way her eyes lit up the next day when he bumped into her, he wasn't quite sure himself, but if he had to pin it to one thing, it was God's will. It was God's will that he returned to Derby Creek after all these years and God had sent the storm so that he could meet his future wife.

"Uri, you're up early," Betty said as she entered the kitchen where he was having his morning tea.

"Jah, up and ready for church," he said and grinned excitedly.

She came to sit next to him and perched her chin on her hand, looking at him all dreamy eyed. Shifting slightly to get some distance, he smiled and shoved the plate of rusks closer to her.

"I'm on my way to collect Rachel for church," he announced, not sure how Betty would react.

From day one, she had made it no secret that she fancied him; neither did Amity, so it was better if he got it out in the open before either of them got their hopes up.

"Rachel?" Betty said scrunching up her face, "Have you asked her then?"

He nodded and took the last sip of his tea, "Jah, she's a shy one, but she accepted my offer."

Betty scratched her head and slumped back in her chair, and Uri could just imagine what thoughts were flitting through her mind, hoping that this would not ruin their friendship. But when Betty stood up and held her hand up for a high-five, he grinned.

"She's a dear friend, but a nervous wreck, you best make sure you treat her right," Betty grinned, "She's had a lot of hardship with that stepmother of hers."

Uri frowned, tempted to ask about this stepmother, but held back. If anyone was going to tell him about Rachel, it was Rachel herself. He would want for no secrets or tall tales to come from anyone other than her.

He looked at the clock against the wall in the kitchen and took his hat, nodded at Betty and headed out. For a man nearing his thirties, he felt like teenager himself.

~*~

Rachel waited outside for Uri's arrival and her stomach was doing wild flips, while her heart was missing beats every so often trying to keep up the pace. She had never entertained the advances of a man, and had no idea how to behave in the presence of one who had made his intensions clear. A boy simply did not offer a girl a ride in his buggy unless he was interested in her as more than a friend. This was serious business. She also omitted to let her father know, because she knew that Elsa would have a hundred and one things to say about it. She shifted on the swing chair changing her position, trying to find the one that made her feel most at ease, but her body felt awkward. Her arms felt as if they were too long, her legs felt numb and overall her body and mind appeared to be disconnected. Tired of trying to figure out the best seating position she stood up and paced up and down the porch, and then finally she opted for leaning against the pillar. Just in time too, as she heard the nearing rumble of a buggy, which could only have been Uri.

When he came to a stop in front of her gate, she quickly rushed down the stairs.

"Morning Rachel, you look lovely today," Uri said as he climbed out and came around to help her in.

"Good morning," she said softly.

"Did you sleep well?"

"Jah, I did, thank you."

It took her some time to loosen up and say more than four words at a time, but Uri had this amazing ability to make her feel free. With him she didn't have to count every word, or watch her tongue. She could just say what she wanted. On their way to church, he asked her about the things she likes most. The talked about her life, and her family, she didn't feel like she needed to hide anything from him at all. She even admitted how she felt about Elsa, which made her feel less restricted. At church, they didn't sit next to each other, but Betty and Amity were curious as ever.

"So he picked you did he?" Amity whispered under her breath.

"I don't know, maybe," Rachel murmured.

"You're blind as a bat; everyone can see he likes you."

Rachel blushed and kept her head down, her friends were impossible and as much as she tried to pay attention to the service she couldn't. If it wasn't for Betty or Amity, whispering to her under their breaths, it was the sure awareness of Uri watching her. And that did not go unnoticed by her friends either.

By the time the service had come to an end, Rachel couldn't wait to get outside to catch a breath of fresh air, and steal a moment for herself, but it was short lived.

"You never told us you're meeting a boy?" Elsa said as she came to stand next to Rachel.

"I didn't know I needed your permission," Rachel said blankly.

"Well I suppose you are old enough to make your own, but you know, Albert will be very disappointed that you never told him."

Rachel knew exactly what Elsa was playing at, and this time she was not going to let the woman who pretends to care throw any hurdles in her way.

"I think he'll live, and you should be too pleased that I won't be a bother to you for much longer."

Talk about rushing into things, Rachel thought as she hurried away from Elsa, it wasn't as if Uri was going to ask for her hand in marriage, they hardly knew each other. But even if that wasn't the case, whatever happened, come the beginning of winter, she would move out anyway and start her own life, with or without a husband.

Chapter 5

Uri had spent most of the time getting to know Rachel, and the more he got to know her, the more he was convinced that she was the perfect wife for him. He had spent almost every evening visiting with Rachel and in the past few months since they started their courtship he got to know a woman, who despite her adversities in life, rose above it all. Her stepmother no longer tried to boss her around, and her father was too pleased that his only daughter is finally blooming.

It was a perfect autumn day; the ground was covered in a carpet of reds and golds that reminded him of Rachel. He had already asked her father for her hand in marriage, and although it didn't quite follow the custom of dating for an extended period, he saw no reason to wait. They were both adults who were in love and certain of one thing, their own happiness.

As usual he waited patiently for Rachel to exit the house, and like two curious toddlers Amity and Betty was not far away either. They had both come to terms with the fact that he had made his choice, and they were extra supportive of Rachel too. As he whispered a silent prayer for guidance, Rachel made her appearance as if the Lord had answered his prayer. Today was the day he was going to ask her for her hand in person.

"Good morning Uri," she said and her smile lit up his world.

"Morning to you Rachel, you look absolutely radiant today," he complemented her and it earned him an even wider smile.

"I made myself a new dress, do you like it?"

"It's beautiful," he said and held out his hand.

He could already imagine the gasps and giggles coming from the two friends as he struggled to find the right words. He had rehearsed it so well, but now here in the moment, he was at a loss for words.

"Are you alright?" she asked and placed the back of her hand against his cheek, "You look flustered."

Uri cleared his throat and caught her hand, keeping it against his cheek, "I'm fine, but there is something I would like to ask you."

Rachel tilted her head and her hazel eyes sparkled with curiosity as she waited for him to speak.

"Go on!" Betty shouted from across the road!

Uri closed his eyes and smiled, they weren't helping him at all.

"Uri?" Rachel said softly, "What is it?"

He took a deep breath, and then took both her hands in his, "Rachel, I have spoken to your father, and I would be honoured if you would agree to become my wife."

The way Rachel's expression changed from being concerned to completely surprise was priceless. She didn't have to answer him at all, because the way her lips tugged into a wide smile and her eyes filled with tears, he knew she wouldn't turn him down.

Rachel flung her arms around his neck and buried her face in the crook of his neck and whispered, "I thought you'd never ask."

Uri chuckled, "I was hoping you would accept."

"Why would I not?" she said and smiled lovingly up at him.

JOANNA

1.

Tracing her finger over the cold, gray tombstone, Joanna inhaled deeply and choked back a sob. Kneeling in the pasture of their family's cemetery, she placed a bouquet of daffodils in front of the stone. It all felt like a dream to her. She didn't think she would ever lose her mother. She was her best friend and now that she was gone Joanna felt lost. She spoke softly to the stone just as she would as if her mother were standing beside her. "Hello, Mother. I miss you more each day. I really wish you could have stayed. It's lonely here without you. Everyone is trying to be strong. They want to continue life as it was before, but without you being here, it's impossible. I know you're in a better place and you're not in pain from the illness ravaging your earthly body, but it's still hard. I just don't know what to do now. I have assumed all of your household duties, just as you would have wished, but I find myself feeling increasingly empty. None of this feels right." Before she could finish her conversation, she heard the distinctive sound of horses clopping in the distance. She knew her brothers would be coming to take her back to their small home in the center of their community. They would have finished their errands in town, and she would be needed soon to start preparing supper. Dusk would be upon them soon, and after evening services, a good meal, a nice fire, and sleep would be arriving soon.

Joanna stood up slowly and ran her fingers along the cold stone one more time, giving a weak smile of recognition to her brother, Eli, who trotted up on his prized horse, Petunia. Petunia was a gentle creature and was easily broken. Eli was good to the creature and she respected him as well, she wouldn't ever buck him off, even when they were traveling through thunderstorms or if she ran up on a snake in the tall weeds. They trusted one another. Joanna could say the same about her brother, even though she was the older sibling, they trusted one another and vowed to always protect one another through all of life's trials. Eli looked down from Petunia and frowned. He hated to see his sister suffer so, but as a young man, he knew that for the good of the community he couldn't let his own sorrows show. He had to be strong for his sister now and show nothing but unconditional support. Now was the time for them to come together as a family and keep each other close. That's what his mother would have wanted. "It's good to see you, sister. Are you ready to return to the house?"

Joanna looked up at Eli's eyes and knew that behind the deep brown spheres, there was a touch of sadness that lingered there. He was trying so hard to put on a brave front, but she knew the truth, he wouldn't be the same after their mother's passing either. "Yes. I'm ready to return, Eli. Can I ride with you?"

"Of course. I think Petunia has it in her to walk us both back home along the path." The horse merely whinnied and they both laughed at her response. As they trotted along the path, Joanna's voice turned solemn once again as she asked, "How's father today?"

"He didn't say much at all, he merely got up and went into his study, where he read some scriptures and made some notes for service, then he walked out into the garden and surveyed the crops. It was like a typical day for him it seems."

"I wish he would express himself more."

"Ah, you know how he is Joanna, that's how he always was, stoic and stone-faced."

"Yeah. Maybe one day we'll figure him out."

"Ha! You have jokes, my sister. I seriously have my doubts about that."

They rode back up to the house in relative silence only listening to the sounds of the birds chirping and the echo of Petunia's hooves against the ground. Reaching the house, the pair dismounted and Eli walked Petunia to the barn, taking care to make sure she had plenty of fresh hay and water. Joanna went straight into the house and immediately made her way to the kitchen. In her mind's eye, she could still see her mother standing by the stove, stirring a pot or leaning over to get a knife from the bottom drawer. It was up to her now to make sure the family was fed. She sighed heavily and reached up above the family's ice box to take down a larger pot which hung above it. It was cast iron and the same one that had been used in the family for generations to make hearty stews and soups. That night Joanna decided she would make the family a hearty beef stew. They had some extra meat frozen already in the icebox and she had plenty of canned vegetables from the summer and fall's gardening. She poured some water that had already been carried inside into the large cast iron pot and lit the fire beneath their wood and coal stove. When it came to a full boil she added the meat and vegetables. Her mother had always tried to make her stews last for a few days and made it a point to ensure it was filling as well. Joanna added some corn starch to thicken the broth and proceeded to flavor it with spices. When her father walked into the kitchen, he hung his head, but then looked up and met Joanna's eyes, giving her a slight nod of approval. When the preparations were finished Joanna carried the pot along with some freshly baked bread out to the dining room. The family took their assigned places around the square table. In their mourning period, it was customary to set an extra place at the table for the lost as well, so her mother's chair while empty next to her father, had a place setting and was served some stew as well. It would be her father's task to consume it.

2.

After all was seated, her father spoke. "Good evening my son and daughter. Let us all rejoice and give thanks for what the day hath brought forth. Now is the time we must graciously give thanks for the abundance the Lord hath provided us with and draw close together as a family in our hour of need. I was reading the scriptures this morning and they brought me much comfort. Despite our loss, I trust each of my children to go on living and continue to be upstanding and show true grace. Now let us break bread and honor the fallen."

They all opened their eyes and lifted their heads watching their father who broke the first bit of bread. He then passed the plate to the others who took their portions and set the tray back in the center of the table. Their meal was eaten in silence and no one dared to speak until their simple supper was finished. Their father then looked at each of them and smiled. Tufts of white hair showed his age and he had a natural ruddiness to his skin tone that made him look jovial. He also had lines etched along his forehead left by the many years of being contemplative. One would look at him and assume he was a stern man all of the time, but he had crows feet and smile lines along his eyelids that told another story. While their father was stern and quiet, Joanna could remember a time when they were children he would play their games with them and tell stories which made all of them laugh joyously. He was a man dedicated to worship, but he also was a man who prided himself on the family he had created.

Rising from the table Joanna began to gather the dishes and place them in the kitchen sink, as she crossed into the other room she heard her father say, "Joanna, I'm very pleased with all the progress you have made in the kitchen with meal preparations. Your mother, rest her soul, would be very proud of you." Tears formed in Joanna's eyes and she bit her bottom lip to choke back a sob. Her mother, Annabelle, had been gone now for over a month, but the loss still stung. Her entire family was stuck living with the reminders of her being. Joanna still hadn't had the heart to clean out her closet or her sewing room. The elders had planned a town gathering at the end of the month, however, so she thought she would take them then and donate them. After all, she was a practical woman, just like her mother before her, and knew that there was no sense in good pieces of clothing going to waste when someone less fortunate could be using them. She responded to her father when returning to the table for a second trip for the remainder of the dishes.

"Thank you father, I appreciate it. I discover more techniques every day. I feel personal growth is important, don't you?"

"Why, of course it is, Joanna. I've watched you and Eli grow through the years and I'm proud of both of you. I personally feel comforted by the fact that no matter how many times I go to complete a task and fail, I always have another opportunity to give it another try. That's the beauty in salvation and forgiveness. As humans, we all fall short of perfection, but there's always the chance to redeem yourself through prayer and multiple attempts."

Eli cleared his throat and spoke for the first time since they arrived home. "I'm glad for that. I know that there have been many times I felt lost or like I was on the wrong path, but I would pray about it and then something would happen or suddenly change in my life." Joanna listened to the pair talk from the kitchen while washing up the supper dishes and smiled. She loved her father and brother dearly but felt lost. She had no one to talk about her daily affairs with now that her mother had passed. She couldn't tell her father about the gossip she overheard while getting notions for sewing. She couldn't talk to her brother about a certain feeling she had in the pit of her stomach when she watched the baker's son splitting wood while hanging their linens out to dry.

She listened as their conversation continued. Her father spoke in a good-natured tone and there was nothing condescending in his voice as he elaborated on the subject matter with his son. "Eli, do you remember that time you came home crying when you were thirteen or fourteen? It was late in the evening and mid-summer. You had just returned from Mrs. Hollister's barn dance, she was having to raise money for the local town orphanage. You came to me and had tears in your eyes and your lips were swollen and shaking. I'll never forget how dejected you looked."

"Yes, father. I remember that well. I had gone to the dance and got quite upset when I saw Pamela Davison dancing with my friend, James."

"Do you remember what I told you?"

"No, I can't say I can recall, though it must have worked, I haven't harbored feelings for Pamela since that night."

"What I told you then son, was that sometimes we think we know what's best for ourselves, but in the end, it's not us who is ultimately in control of that. Our actions may influence our day to day activities, but it is only through faith we can fulfill our ultimate destiny. Our almighty father wants us to be happy, but sometimes we have to learn a lesson the hard way so we don't pursue other things. Your courtship with Pamela, for example, is one of those things. Do you know what she's doing now?"

"No, father. I haven't a clue."

"She decided to go live among the outsiders. Her life has not been beneficial from it, given my understanding. The last news we received in a letter that she decided to pursue her career as a professional dancer. It turns out that career path led her to work in a nightclub for exotic dancing and she's developed a drug addiction. It's in my best estimation that she will more than likely spend a great deal of her life in prison for drug related crimes or prostitution. So, son, as you can see sometimes our Father doesn't answer our prayers for a reason."

"What if I could have changed her? If she stayed with me, then maybe she would have just lived her life pursuing the path of righteousness."

"Well, I know how susceptible young men are to the wiles of women and their charms. I think that given the choice, you would have left and gone with her and been corrupted by the outside world as well. Outside of our community, there is a temptation to pursue wrongdoing on every corner. No matter what your vice, there is some way to purchase it or attain it there. Never forget that on your travels, Eli."

"I won't Father."

3.

Joanna listened to their conversation while she continued to tidy up the dinner dishes. She knew that her mother would have loved that their father was attempting to socialize with his children, but she also knew that her mother would have played devil advocate in the conversation. She wasn't like most of the other women in the town. She was outspoken and often had heated debates on matters of faith or business with her father, yet they worked to balance each other out very well. Joanna was convinced that when God made her mother, his creation was done purely to spite her father and keep him in line.

She cleaned up the sink and then decided she would go ahead and get the percolator ready for the morning's coffee. She knew that would be the first thing their father would ask for when he woke up in the morning. He often preferred the strong brew first thing, then would go out to complete his chores, foregoing breakfast until their animals had been fed. He always said that if one took care of the animals, they would, in turn, take care of you. He lived by this strict routine day in and day out, with little variation in routine, save for the day he celebrated his wedding anniversary with his wife. On that day, both their father and mother would take a rare trip to town, where they would return with not only small gifts for the children but some goods, that were less costly to purchase such as new blades for the farming equipment. Joanna always dreamed of the outside world as being some type of magical realm where everyone had access to things like running water and life was easy, but as she grew older she realized the outsiders weren't much different than those in her own community. She wasn't allowed to do much traveling into town, but when she did she just noticed that the outsiders seemed to base their own value on their material belongings. This concept just simply didn't exist in her community, everything was shared.

Joanna saw that it was dark now outside and with her chores attended to, she didn't see the point in staying with the menfolk talking around the dinner table. Drying her hands on a dish towel, she decided to go ahead and excuse herself. Walking around the side of the table she approached her father and placed her hand on the side of his chair then leaned over kissing him on the forehead. "I'm going to go ahead and turn in for the evening, father. The nightly chores are all completed."

"Ah, yes, very good little one. My precious daughter. You have sweet dreams and remember that your father and brother are here if you have night terrors."

"Oh, papa. I love you. I haven't had a night terror, though, since I was seven years old."

"Still.. think good thoughts."

"I will. Goodnight. Goodnight Eli."

"Goodnight, sister, remember I love you even in your slumber."

"I will."

Joanna walked to her bedroom and lit the small candle that was on her nightstand, it provided enough light to read by, which is the only thing she enjoyed doing in the evenings to relax. Taking off her bonnet, she sat on the edge of the bed and began undoing the long braids she had in her hair. She preferred to keep it pulled up and away from her face during the course of the day since she was often doing chores. The tresses undid themselves easily and she fluffed hands through it, taking her hairbrush and running it through her long brown locks. After she put on her nightgown and hung her daytime dress back up in her standing closet, she picked up her Bible, seeing the notes she had made in the margins. She had been studying a chapter in Revelations that her father recommended. He felt that it would benefit the family to examine the reasons for death together, so they could make some sense of their mother's unexpected passing. She sighed and remembering her place decided she would finish reading and analyzing the chapter when she arose the following morning. Instead, she picked up the paperback she had borrowed from the town's library. It had a handsome cowboy on the front of it and he appeared in front of a herd of galloping horses. He was holding a blonde woman in his arms and she was swooning. Joanna smiled as the opened the book to the place she left off. It wasn't customary for women in her community to read much at all, but she enjoyed the thoughts of romance and found nothing wrong with dreaming about a handsome cowboy of her own. She finished the chapter and blew out her candle, reclining on her twin bed and closing her eyes sleeping almost immediately.

4.

As the dawn peeked through the clouds, Joanna was awakened by Eli, barging into her bedroom unannounced. He let the door bang on the hinges and had a panicked look on his face, as Joanna pulled the covers up over herself asked, "Why, Eli?! Whatever is the matter?! Is it Father?! Is he okay?!"

"Yes. Oh, Joanna, I'm worried. It's Petunia. She's fallen ill I'm afraid. Can you come out to the barn?"

Breathing out a sigh of relief, Joanna nodded and said, "Of course dear brother. Don't be fearful. The Lord will protect Petunia. Give me a few moments to get decent and I will be out there." Joanna calmly got up from her bed and walked to her closet, taking a few moments to pull her hair back and put on her bonnet then putting on her daytime dress. She pulled the laces tight on her boots and hurried out to the barn where she could see Eli standing by Petunia's stall pacing anxiously. "Thank you for coming out sister. I can't figure out what's wrong with her. She won't respond to my coaxing and she's just lethargic. I've never seen her in this state."

"Calm yourself, Eli. Your panicked state is doing her no good either. Animals can sense your fear." Joanna walked up to the mare who was laying down and looked into Petunia's deep brown eyes. She then placed her hand gently on the creature's forehead. She then stroked the animal's head and back, making soothing sounds, just as her mother would do them when they were sick youngsters. "Yes. You're right to have come to fetch me. She's definitely fallen ill. Let's just hope its a bug. Father has a trip planned to go into town to gather some new ax blades for the fall cutting. I'll go with him and stop by the library and see if I can find a cure in some of the veterinary medicine books they have shelved. Don't worry, brother. We will do what we can for her. Just be fervent in your prayers and there will be a way delivered."

Joanna walked back into the home and began preparing her father's morning coffee. Daylight had just broke and she knew he would be happy to get the day started like normal. When he walked in the kitchen he smiled seeing her standing at the stove as her mother would have, fixing his coffee and preparing breakfast for her brother. Eli always had a voracious appetite She set the steaming mug in front of him and said, "Good morning, Father. I must confess it's already been eventful."

"Oh, really how so?"

"It seems Petunia has fallen ill. I was hoping it would be okay if I went with you while you were in town today to look up some medicine for her at the library."

"I certainly hate to hear that Petunia has taken a turn for the worse. She has been good to our little family. I think that's a wonderful idea darling. God can work miracle cures, but only if we're willing to do a bit of the work as well. After the morning feeding, we will go into town. Be prepared. While I'm purchasing the new blades for the fall wood harvest, you can look into a cure for our Petunia. I bet your brother is worried sick."

"Oh, he is Father. You know he's always been close to the mare."

"We shall do what we can. Thank you for the finely brewed cup of coffee. Now I must get to work, the daylight is already streaming upon us and the chickens will be happy to receive their breakfast."

"Thank you, Father."

Joanna finished making the biscuits and gravy for breakfast then poured them all glasses of freshly squeezed orange juice from the assortment of oranges that they had traded for in town earlier in the summer. She knew their shelf life would be expiring soon and didn't want anything to go to waste. Waste not, want not, her mother always said. She also knew that they all need to keep their strength up because as soon as they got back from town the entire community would gather and chop wood for their collective heat in the winter. After completing her chores and cleaning up the cooking utensils she set the meal on the dining room table and gathered her bag for their trip into town. She made certain she had her city library card and decided to take her paperback with her and exchange it for another as it was nearing completion anyway. Looking around the empty room she sighed. She was worried about her brother, but also she felt a doubt creeping into her soul and a generalized discomfort, wondering if this is how the remainder of her days would be spent, taking care of her father and brother , never knowing the love of a man or having her own family to raise.

Her father and brother came back into the house after feeding the animals and sat down at the table, nodding in appreciation at having their meal already set before them. Eli spoke then, asking to say the morning prayers and included a blessing for his favorite mare as well. They ate the rest of their meal in silence and Joanna immediately went to the sink and began cleaning up the dishes, so she wouldn't have to do both the breakfast and dinner dishes before bed. She also was anticipating having a busy day tending to Petunia upon their return. Her father came and got her when the horses were hitched up to the wagon and her brother helped her climb in beside him. Her father gave his horses a quick pat on the head and they departed on their journey into town.

5.

Arriving in the nearest town, Joanna took in her surroundings as her father hitched up the wagon to the hitching post by the hardware store. She got out of the buggy, amidst the stares of the townspeople. She imagined she looked quite strange to then in her pale blue day dress, with her hair pinned up in a bonnet, while her father was dressed head to toe in all black, complete with his wide-rimmed black hat. His long brown beard wasn't shaved, merely groomed and it did betray his age, as spots of gray could be seen in it when the sun hit it just right. He spoke briefly to his daughter before going inside the store. "Remember daughter, be polite to the townspeople, but do not engage in lengthy conversation unless it pertains to spreading the Gospel. I will be here when you are ready to leave but try to find the information you seek quickly. I suspect this lost time will hurt our productivity later and we won't be able to get as much done as we should. Be careful, Joanna."

Joanna nodded and hugged her father before crossing the street and rounding the block heading to the library. She cast her eyes downward mostly only looking up periodically to dodge obstacles. She opened the doors to the city library and the pleasant librarian smiled and waved at her when she entered. She smiled back and returned the greeting. She liked the librarian, who never questioned her when she came in even as a little girl clutching her mother's skirts. The older clerk would give her lollipops when her mother checked out her religious books and romance novels. Now Joanna was grown and even though she didn't get a lollipop, she still felt those warm feelings when she was in the library. She walked up to the desk and quietly dropped her book on the counter. "I need to return this, and I will be getting another one if I can find the other information I need in time."

"Sure thing, Joanna. Have you been doing okay, since your mother's passing?"

"Oh, yes we have been doing alright, thank you. I'm sorry I was in such a bad state when you saw me last. I am adjusting to this new normal."

"Well, that's good. If you need anything, you let me know as always."

"I will. I will see you when I return."

Joanna then walked off, smiling once more at the clerk. She rounded the corner to the reference desk where there was no clerk, but there was a younger looking man in grease-stained coveralls standing by the finance books, looking bewildered. Joanna watched him pull out a book from the shelf as the rest came tumbling down. She couldn't stifle a small giggle as he fumbled trying to catch them all. He turned around hearing her laughter and she was met with a sheepish smile and the most striking blue eyes she'd ever seen. He took her by surprise as she felt her heart beat faster within her chest and suddenly heat rose to her face as she blushed deeply. Before she could say a word he smiled broadly at her and said, "They don't make these shelves the way they used to do they?"

Joanna giggled once again and said, "No. They certainly don't."

"I don't really know much about this place. I needed a book on taxes, I own my own mechanic shop and I'm doing my own this year to save money for the business. Maybe I should have just paid someone."

"Well, what are you looking for? Maybe I can help."

"A book to tell me how to do it."

Joanna paused for a moment surveying the shelves then reached down to the bottom one, accidently brushing the man's hand as she picked up a hefty volume and placed it in his arms. "Here you go. This will guide you through the process."

"Oh wow. Thank you. I appreciate that ma'am. It's nice to meet you, my name's David."

"I'm Joanna. I'm not from around here, as you can tell."

David took a step toward her, closing the distance, and Joanna felt a certain electricity pass through them. She let the heat rise to her cheeks again and once more looked into his blue eyes. He was in good shape and looked strong from his work. He had blonde hair and was clean shaven. He didn't look like any of the men from their community, but he did seem to possess the same kindness behind his eyes and good spirit. He responded by saying, "I wish you were from around here. I'd hire you to do my taxes."

She chuckled at his joke, then suddenly remembered her purpose. "I really hate to cut on conversation short, David, but I have to get some information then return to my community, my brother's horse is sick and needs medical attention I know nothing of."

"Oh, I'm sorry to hear that. Maybe I can help. I grew up on a ranch."

She couldn't believe her ears. She had wanted a cowboy all of her own. Could it be that her prayers had been answered? He seemed so genuine and caring. She explained the problem with Petunia and David gave her the information she needed to attend to the mare. He reassured her it was nothing major that some tender loving care couldn't fix. He then went on to say that his specialty in life was fixing broken things. Joanna considered the gravity of his statement before turning to leave and decided to do something she would need to ask forgiveness for later.

"You have been so helpful David, could I have your address?"

"Only if I can have yours too."

The pair exchanged addresses and Joanna exited the library, turning around to see David staring at her making her exit. She didn't know what had come over her, but she knew in her heart this man was her destiny.

6.

She exited the library to find her father standing red-faced by the door, checking his pocket watch. She hadn't realized how much time had passed talking with David, she only knew that it felt like they had known each other a lifetime. Feeling the need to apologize she spoke to her father, when they crossed to the buggy, "I'm sorry, father. It took me longer to get the information I needed than what I thought."

He didn't say anything, but merely nodded and coaxed the horses out of the lot and towards the path back to their community. Her father finally spoke when they were close to the halfway point between town and their village. "You know why we caution each other when talking with townspeople? It's not because our religion has restrictions on being social and making friends. In fact, we are encouraged to witness to everyone we possibly can. It's because not all people are righteous, Joanna. Not everyone will have your best interest at heart, and the original evil does find its way into the hearts of men. Some of the people you encounter in the outside world, well let's say the majority of them, only are interested in preying on the weak. It's their life's goal, not helping others or doing good."

Joanna turned her eyes downward again as her father patted her on the leg continuing, "Remember, no matter what happens, Joanna, your family will always support you within the community. We, however, could not help you should you decide to live among the outsiders. You would be shunned and on your own, you know it's our way, there's no changing that." Joanna nodded in acknowledgment, silently rubbing the piece of paper in her pocket which had David's address on it. She knew in her heart, that she needed to see the mysterious cowboy mechanic once again, but didn't like the idea of her father's disapproval. He would never allow such a thing, she felt conflicted and sick at heart the entire way home.

Arriving back at the community they were greeted by Eli, whose worried look had only grown more exasperated during their time away. "Greetings, Father. Greetings, Sister. Did you acquire the knowledge you sought?"

"I did brother. Let's go to the barn and see what we can do."

Together they walked to the barn and checked on Petunia. Joanna took care to follow David's precise instructions and administered a careful mixture of salt brine and water to the mare who greedily lapped it up. It had seemed that she had just gotten a bit dehydrated during their previous days' activities and was feeling under the weather. They monitored her condition throughout the day and it did improve as she eventually got up and started wandering back and forth in her stall, anxious for a trot. In addition to that the new blade purchase, expedited the wood cutting process and the community made short work of the wood pile, stockpiling enough wood to last the entire winter in half the time it normally would. They decided as a community to celebrate their recent accomplishment and give thanks to the Lord, with a feast to be held that upcoming Saturday night.

Joanna spent the night quietly in her room after supper and allowed herself to think of David. She knew beyond a shadow of a doubt that she needed him in her life. She believed, despite her father's warnings that there were good and decency in his soul. No one without a good heart, would have freely given her that information she needed to help her animal. Most of the outsiders would have offered their services and charged a pretty penny for such knowledge. Joanna thought of the feast Saturday and sighed. Did she want to be stuck in the community all her life, eventually marrying a man who had little passion for anything in life? It was then Joanna made her decision. She would slip away during the barn dance on Saturday and go see David.

As the community was abuzz with the festivities at the dance on Saturday night, Joanna excused herself to go back to the house, hugging her brother and her father tightly before exiting, saying she felt ill and needed to call it an early night. Unnoticed by anyone else in the community, she then proceeded down the well-worn path and made her way to town. She made her way to the address David had scrawled on a ripped piece of an envelope from his coveralls and knocked on his door.

David opened the door, rubbing his eyes, apparently awakened by her rapping. He was groggy but smiled broadly in recognition. "Joanna, is that you are am I dreaming?"

"No. You're not dreaming, David. I'm really here." She paused a moment, considering her options. She thought for a moment about what advice her mother would give her in this moment. She thought back to when she was a little girl clutching on to her mother's skirt, frightened by some imaginary threat. She would have said, "Ah, my precious little girl, there is nothing to be afraid of but your own imagination. If you don't give your fear power over you, you can achieve anything you want in this lifetime." Joanna hesitated a moment then said to David all while blushing and smiling, "I came to be with you David, and hopefully one day be your wife."

David took Joanna by the hand and led her over his front stoop, making sure she didn't trip over the door sill on the way in. When he shut the door behind her he pulled her into his arms and kissed her deeply. Joanna felt a joy like none other she had felt in her life, spread through her bones and body. He then looked deeply into her eyes and said, "Well. I'm not the smartest man you will ever know, nor will I ever be the ideal of perfection, but I promise you this Joanna. I am a decent man with a good heart, and I promise to make this life the best we can possibly have together. So, yes. I do want you to stay with me. You're all I've thought about since I met you that day at the library, and you're all I want to think about for the rest of my days." The pair then walked hand in hand into David's modest living room where they sit side by side on the sofa, holding each other until they drifted off peacefully.

FANNIE : AN AMISH WIDOW

MAYA MILLER

79

After the children were asleep was always the worst time of day for Fannie. That was the time when she had time to think. She had time to worry. She had time to grieve. Peter's death had been an unexpected blow. They had plans. They had a way of life worked out that would support them into old age, and allow their children to grow up comfortable and safe. And then one day it was all taken away from her in the blink of an eye.

She still winced and did a mental check of where all six of her children were at that moment each time there was a knock on the front door. She wondered if that would ever stop. Would the lack of another adult presence in the house ever seem less foreign to her? His smell still lingered in the closets, full of the clothes that she had not yet had the heart to give away. Small reminders, like jars of his favorite pickles that no one else in the house could stand, would jump out at her when she least expected it. And now everything was so very hard. Her mother and her friend, Katie, from next door did all that they could to help. She really should not have felt as overwhelmed as she did with everything that the community was doing to help her family cope, but she just was.

She was tired, shell-shocked by how different each of her children was reacting to the death of their father. Pete Jr. was sixteen and had always been the responsible, care-taking second-hand to his father. He was now spending as little time as possible at home or with his family. Albert, her fourteen-year-old, who had always been very quiet and calm, had taken to yelling at his younger siblings for any annoyance, real or perceived. May, her thirteen-year-old, was growing up too quickly, though the fear and debilitating grief gripping her were obvious. Conrad, her eleven-year-old, had always idolized his brother Albert, and now, more than before, was following in his footsteps with yelling and impatience dictating much of his day. Robert, her nine-year-old, was starting to act out and get into trouble at school, something that had never happened before. And her youngest,

Madeline, had morphed into a seven-year-old automaton. She had always been vivacious and lively, but since Peter's death she barely said "boo" to anyone. None of her children were acting like the children she had known a year ago, and Fannie was scared. Maybe that was what it came down to. She was terrified. She didn't know if she could stand up in the face of so much loss and tragic change. The savings that she and Peter had tried to build up over the years was shrinking, and none too slowly. All the extra work that the community was steering her way was just not making ends meet. It wasn't enough. No matter how she coped and moved on, which is what she was desperately trying to do, getting back on her feet was going to require a Herculean effort and a lot of changes. Peter was gone, and her dwelling on her own heartbreak was going to mean disaster for her children. They needed her, and she needed to be strong. But when all was quiet, she allowed herself the indulgence of tears – tears for Peter, tears for herself, tears for her children, and tears to hopefully wash the fear away.

* * *

"Fannie!" Her mother's voice roused her from a dreamless sleep. The night before had turned into early morning before Fannie's body had finally let her fall asleep. She had heard the roosters next door crowing at the sunrise as she had drifted off, tucked as far to her side of the bed as possible. But now it was morning, her mother was here and she needed to get her children ready to go. With a stretch and a yawn, she slowly sat up and then rubbed her hands roughly over her face to wake herself up. "Fannie, darling?" Her mother's voice came from outside her room this time, as the door pushed open with a creak.

"Good morning, Mama."

"Hello, darling. Did you sleep okay?" The corners of her mother's eyes were tight.

"What's wrong, Mama? She sat up quickly, completely alert now. "Is everything okay with you and Dad?" Along with all of the fear of something happening to her children since Peter's death came the fear of something happening to her parents. She didn't know if she could take any more hurt or loss at that point.

"Oh, now, calm yourself, my child. We are just fine. The children are just fine – already off to school. You just sit back and rest a bit more while you tell me about the plans for today."

"Wait, Mama, what do you mean that the children are all off to school? What time is it?" There was a sinking feeling in her stomach. She'd done it again.

"It's 9:30."

Fannie groaned and put her head in her hands.

"Well, you were sleeping when I arrived and I saw Kathryn outside, so I called her over and we got the children roused, fed, dressed and off to school to let you sleep."

"Oh, Mama, I wish that you'd woken me up. I promised May that I would stop staying in bed all day. She must be terrified that I'm falling back into a depression." Her stomach was flip-flopping and her face burned. She was panicked. Her daughter May so hard, and when Fannie had fallen into a deep depression for nearly three weeks after his death, May was the one that finally had the courage to come into her room and yell at her, reminding her that she was a mother, that Pete Jr., Albert and May might have been old enough t take care of themselves, but Conrad, Robert and Madeline needed her. They were so young, and so scared. Her staying in bed all day was unfair to them.

"Mom, we've all lost Daddy, but you are our only hope for getting back to a normal life. Please don't abandon us." Fannie would never forget how it had felt to hear those words from her thirteen-year-old daughter's mouth. It was a mix of shame for her own behavior, surprise at the level of anger from her daughter, and pride in what an amazing young woman May was already growing into.

"My love, you are wise beyond your years," she has told her through tears, as she grabbed her close for a hug. "I promise I won't do this again." May had simply nodded, hugged her back and left the room, saying "I laid out a dress for you to put on for breakfast."

And that had been the end of it. Nearly a year had now passed and she had not once missed breakfast, unless she had to leave early to deliver a completed project – and those times were always planned. And today she had broken her promise. Her heart fluttered as regret hit her solidly in the chest.

"Fannie, don't worry. Kathryn and I were together before the children were up and we agreed that we would just act as if this was planned. You have been working awfully hard lately with all of the extra jobs, and we told the children that you just needed a morning of rest. They trust you. They know you are doing your best. May is grieving her father's death, but as long as you are there when she needs you, it will all be fine. I am proud of how you are holding your head high in the face of everything."

Fannie stared at her mother. She had never heard such praise from her. In fact, she always assumed that the reason that her mother was so helpful since Peter's death was that she believed her daughter would never be able to cope or maintain a life for the children on her own. It never occurred to her that her mother might be proud of her. She couldn't think of any words to say in response to her mother's unusually heart-felt sentiments, so she simply nodded and said "okay, let's tackle today."

"I'll give you a few minutes to gather yourself," her mother said as she left the room.

Fannie dressed quickly, taking several deep breaths to calm her nerves. It had not occurred to her how much it mattered in her heart how her children felt about her. It had not registered up until now that the one thing that was really keeping her going forward everyday was making sure that her children would be able to lead happy, healthy lives. They all needed to get through this hard time, but her goal was to bring them out the other side with her right there to carry them through anything else that life might hand them. They couldn't do that if they didn't trust her.

With a final look in the mirror as she straightened her dress on her now thinner-than-they-used-to-be shoulders, she gave a final sigh and headed down the hall toward the kitchen. And as she rounded the corner she let out a small squeak. The kitchen was a mess.

"Katie," she breathed as an oath.

Her good friend and neighbor Katie, or Kathryn as her mother insisted upon calling her, was nothing short of a Godsend. She had been there since the moment that Fannie had found out the news about Peter. She helped care for the kids. She went out and urged people to send more projects Fannie's way. But there was one thing that Fannie couldn't count on Katie for, and that was cleaning up after herself. Every time Katie was over to care of the kids, especially if there was food preparation involved, the place would be trashed. Katie's house looked the same way. Being neat and tidy was just not something Katie included in her list of talents.

"So, Kathryn did leave a bit of cleaning to do," Fannie's mother said with a shrug.

Fannie chuckled, and the accompanying smile felt like it stretched her facial muscles. "*How odd*," she thought, and reached up to put her hands on her cheeks. "*Do I really smile so seldom?*" She looked around and saw that the shades were shut, casting one big shadow around the whole kitchen.

"Shall we get this cleaned up before I go?" Her mother smiled encouragingly.

"You know what, mom," Fannie said, feeling a strong need for quiet, "I think that I am going to tackle this on my own this morning. I am in between jobs and I have plenty of time before the children get home. I want to put some love into it."

Fannie's mother stared at her for a long moment and then, unsuccessfully trying to hide her smile, she said "very well. I will stop in later to check-in on you once the children are home from school." That was what Fannie loved most about her mother; she didn't feel the need to say everything that came into her head. She obviously had some emotional reaction to Fannie's declaration that she wanted to put some love back into her home, but she kept it to herself and just let the moment happen.

Once the door shut and Fannie was on her own, she put on her apron, rolled up her sleeves and enthusiastically got to work. She didn't know how long the energy and motivation was going to last, so she figured that she might as well take advantage of it before she regretted sending her mother away. She opened the shades and let in the bright morning sun. She opened the windows and breathed in the crisp air. The she began in earnest to tackle the mess that Katie had left her.

Nearly an hour later, the kitchen was shining and fresh and she felt better about her space than she had in a long time. For some reason, the fact that she had come so close to disappointing May had lit a fire under her, so to speak, and she wanted her children to come home and feel proud of what she had accomplished that day, and safe in the knowledge that their mother would be caring for them and their home.

A knock sounded on the door, and Fannie's stomach did its usual flip-flop. But before she could sink too deeply into worry that it was someone coming to her with bad news about her children, she recognized Katie's voice. "Fannie? You in here?" The door opened slowly, and Katie sheepishly peaked around the corner.

"Hey, Katie. Come on in."

"I know, I know. You must be livid. I'm so so so so so so sorry about the mess I left. After the kiddos were on their way, I had to run home to do some stuff. I told your mom I would be back. I bet she never told you that, did she?"

Fannie smiled. "Why would I be livid? You saved me this morning. My mom said the children had no idea that I had just slept in like I had no responsibilities. I can't thank you enough."

Katie, who was not particularly comfortable with shared feelings and what she called "mushy displays," waved Fannie off and walked to the refrigerator, helping herself to some juice. There was a loud bang outside and then a rhythmic hammering began, the sound carrying in through the open window.

"Who is that, Katie? Are some of the men working on your house?"

"No," Katie grinned. "That's the newcomer to the neighborhood. He lives two houses down, on my other side. He's been here about three months. Have you really never noticed him?"

Fannie was surprised to hear that someone new had been living so close and she had not even noticed. Prior to Peter's death, she would have been the first one over there with a basket of baked goods to welcome him to the community. She looked up at Katie and registered just how much grinning she was doing. "What is making you so giddy?"

"Oh nothing," Kate sing-songed.

Fannie shrugged. She was used to her friend sometimes being a little silly or hard to read. "So what's the new guy like? What does he bring to the community?"

"Well, let's see. He is young, maybe our age. He is unmarried, with no children. As far as I know he has never been married. He has good skills with building and farm-tending that will contribute well here. And," she added excitedly, "he is absolutely one of the most handsome men that I have ever seen..."

"Ahh." Now Fannie understood what all of the grinning was about. Katie always loved to be the first to discover something beautiful, and beautiful men were her absolute favorite, even if she was happily married.

"He's taller than my father and darker than me. He is kind to the community children, works hard to help out, and I hear that besides all of these gifts, he can cook ad enjoys the company of family.

Fannie was suspicious of her friend suddenly. "Why are you telling me all of this?"

"I just think that he's a good man and a valuable addition to our community."

That seemed like a reasonable response from anyone but Katie. Fannie knew better. "Oh, please, Katie. That kind of thing doesn't matter to you. What are you really up to? You aren't trying to set me up with another man, are you?" Suddenly, the amusement that she had been feeling morphed into annoyance, and then downright anger. "I was a wife. I have had my children. I am a widow now, not a wife. That is who I am."

Katie looked at her friend levelly for a few quiet moments. "Oh, Fannie, I am so sorry that you feel that way. You're young. I'm not saying that you need to marry *this* man, but there is no reason that you can't marry *some* man *someday*. I was just trying to point out to you that there are men out there worth knowing. There are men out there worth having. Once your heart is healed, I'm just hoping that you can find a way to open it up again."

Fannie was silent as she tried to hold back the hot tears that prickled behind her eyes. She nodded. It was the best that she could do. No one had spoken to her so frankly about moving on in her romantic life since Peter's death, and it was a shock to her to consider that it could ever actually happen. On the contrary, most people referred to her as "Peter's widow," and she figured that was who she would always be.

"I'm only going to say two other things, and then I will let it go for now." Katie reached out and grabbed Fannie's hand. First...you are not dead, so please make sure that you let yourself live the rest of your life. Thrive, don't just survive." Her eyes bore into Fannie's as she let that statement hang in the air between them. Then in true Katie fashion, her eyes flashed with a hint of mischief, and the corners of her lips quirked up in a small grin. "Second...John is a very handsome man. At least let yourself look and see what is possible."

"Oh, you..." Fannie started to say, but was overcome by emotions. Her friend was amazingly supportive and always had her best interest at heart. Maybe she had a point. Maybe just allowing her mind to entertain the idea of moving on in love might not be the worst thing ever.

"I've got to get going." Katie gave Fannie a big hug and smiled. She walked to the kitchen hooks to retrieve her belongings while Fannie returned to cleaning the kitchen. Suddenly, a surprised squeak filled the kitchen. "Why, hello, John. It's nice to see you, but I am on my way out."

Fannie had frozen with her back still to the door. A deep voice answered "Excuse me, Miss Kathryn. It's nice to see you again. I am here to see Miss Fannie. I believe that I might have some work for her and the community elders suggested that I come to discuss the matter with her."

"Fannie, someone is here to see you." Fannie could hear the smile in her friend's voice. She didn't need to look and blush at the extra attention.

"Thank you, Katie." She turned around and was rendered speechless by the person that she saw in front of her. He was tall with strong-looking arms and legs. His hair and eyes were dark, and his skin was sun-kissed where it was not covered by well-worn work clothes. His gaze was intense, but kind, and his facial features seemed to be carved or chiseled, rather than made of blood and flesh. With a start, she realized that she had been staring, and the kind smile and expression that had graced this man's face before were now being replaced by a look of awkward confusion.

"Miss Fannie, I presume?" He said slowly.

Fannie shook her head, attempting to shake off the sudden and unexpected reaction that she was feeling in her body. She was not allowed to be attracted to a man so soon after the death of her husband. Was she? "Yes, sorry. You surprised me is all. May I have the pleasure of your name, sir?"

"Yes, of course. Please forgive my manners. My name is John Miller. I live down the street, on the other side of your friend, Miss Katie."

"Hello Mr. Miller. Katie was just telling me that you had moved to the community a few weeks ago. Welcome." She knew that she should invite him in and ask him to sit down for some refreshment, but she was just too weary of the reaction that she was having to John Miller to allow him to get too comfortable. "How can I help you today? I heard you mention something to Katie about some work?"

"Please call me John, Miss Fannie. I'm here with an offer of some steady work for the next few months, maybe half a year. I have been contracted to work on a home in the next town over. It is not one of our community homes, but they have a distinct appreciation for our craftsmanship and style. Some of the requests that they have made fall into your area of expertise, so I have been told. They are asking for couch covers, curtains and throw pillows that will match what they have envisioned for their home, as well as other home textiles. They would also like several Amish dolls for their children's rooms and guest rooms. I am building and repairing parts of the house, both on the inside and the outside, and they want someone like you to make it pleasing to the eye. Would you have time for a project like that?"

As John finished telling her about the project, Fannie blushed. She realized that while she had taken in what he had said, she had actually been more interested in admiring the way that his lips moved and the muscles in his body shifted as he gestured about what he was describing. "Umm, yes of course," she stammered. "That sounds like a project I would very much enjoy doing.

John smiled and Fannie caught her breath. He had a luminous smile. "All right, then. We will meet here at nine o'clock tomorrow morning to head over for a meeting with the family."

Suddenly uneasy, Fannie said, "I'm sorry?"

"Didn't I mention that they would like the work done at their home, both mine and yours? That way they have more 'creative control' as they put it."

"But, I..." she trailed off, trying to find words for all of the doubts that had suddenly fallen into her mind. Besides the logistical concerns of working in someone else's house, there was the guilt and the discomfort of spending time with another man so soon after Peter's death, especially a man that she obviously found attractive.

"Of course, you are concerned. My apologies. I left out some vital details. The wife has a fully functional sewing and work room. They already have purchased material from the Millers in our community store. Also, they will provide us transportation because they know that you need to be home for your children and we do not have vehicles. I worked those details out already."

Fannie nodded. That would solve all of the logistical concerns that she had, but the emotional ones...that was going to be far more complicated. "Okay, John. I will see you tomorrow morning." And with a shy smile, she led him out the door and closed it behind him. Then she closed her eyes, praying that she had made the right decision.

* * *

"Albert, it's your evening to say grace," Fannie said as she, her six children and Katie all sat down to dinner that evening.

"I would say grace happily if Robert would stop kicking my leg under the table," he replied sourly.

"I'm not kicking you!" the younger boy yelled.

"Yes you are," barked Conrad.

"Children, please stop bickering. Albert, please say grace." Fannie could feel her face getting hot in frustration. Dinners with Peter had always been a time for the children to chatter pleasantly away about their day, as they vied for their father's attention. Now she was lucky if she could get a word out of any of them that was not bickering or complaining. A wave of stomach-sinking sadness washed over Fannie and she felt her shoulders droop.

"Al, please, big man." Katie's smile and gentle voice did the trick. Albert nodded and reluctantly said grace.

"How was school today, children?" Fannie asked when he was finished, hoping that it would start the children talking like they used to.

"Well," Albert started, "May broke down in tears because she couldn't figure out her work; Robert was sent to the corner, AGAIN; Madeline never talks to anyone; I cannot stand any of the kids my age; Conrad can't seem to get along with anyone except me, and I find his following me around annoying,; and Pete doesn't even talk to us when we're there together. Anything else you want to know, Mom?"

"Albert!" Katie said, her face mirroring the shock on Fannie's. "You need to think about how you speak to your mother. Do you think God... do you think your father would be pleased to hear that tone and those harmful and spiteful words spoken at your family table?"

Albert's gaze remained on the table, and his lips pursed. He was not used to reprimands from Katie. It obviously stung. Fannie was speechless. It occurred to her that she might not be able to pull her children back from these new paths, as much as she wanted to.

They all ate in silence for a few minutes and then Fannie heard "forgive me, mama." The words were so quiet she thought that she'd imagined them. But when she looked up, she saw that the entire table was looking at Albert, who was gazing at her. His eyes were the same as they had been when he was a baby, though he was now fourteen. And in them, she saw the hurt reflected that she and the whole family felt. She held out her arms and he got up and came to her for a long hug, like he hadn't done in months. And just like that, her hope that they would be alright was restored.

For the rest of that dinner, they did not happily chatter away like they used to do with their father, but they actually held conversations, and even Pete Jr. was somewhat engaged. Maybe Albert's outburst was the crack in the dam that they needed to finally start to heal.

* * *

The next day went by very quickly for Fannie. After the breakthrough with her children the night before, she was feeling more optimistic and productive. She hadn't realized the scope of the worry that she had been harboring for her children and her family until she had seen what could actually be positive changes. She met John, as they had planned, at nine o'clock, and they took the transportation provided by the family to the home. It was a large home, but not as imposing as some in the neighborhood. She and John set straight to work – he outside, and she in the surprisingly well stocked and organized sewing and work room.

Fannie found it pleasant to have her mind so occupied with something other than worry. For the first time in many months, she found her rhythm with her work, and was producing some of her best quality product since before Peter's death.

She took a couple of stretch breaks throughout the day and sat for a very pleasant lunch, in companionable silence with John, on the patio behind the home. She had thought that spending the time with a strange man would be awkward and she would need to find empty words to fill in the space until they went back to work. But that was not the case at all. In fact, she found his mere presence to be a comfort and a pleasure. Every once in a while the wind would shift and she would catch a waft of his male scent, and she would close her eyes, inhaling just a bit deeper.

* * *

Fannie's next few weeks continued in very much the same way. The money that she was making at the job was allowing her some breathing room with finances, and she was doing such good work that the family had promised to refer other local friends to her and John for work on their homes. She and John would make the trip to their worksite each morning and work hard, but separately throughout the day. The only time, besides the travel, that they spent together was at lunch. At first they continued spending the time in simple, silent company. But as the days passed they began conversing about their work, or the community. Then they moved onto topics like where John was from, or how it was for Fannie to grow up in their community. Fannie found herself looking forward to lunch time as the days passed. Having a friendship with John that was not shadowed by her husband's loss or the changes that she had made in her life from wife to widow was refreshing and easy. It was a rest for her heart and her mind. And amazingly, over time, she felt her days begin to lighten, even when she was involved in family or financial matters that were connected to her loss. He never asked questions that she did not want to answer, and he would not call her out if she was guarded in sharing personal details.

"Fannie, I want to ask you something," John said one day about six weeks into their project. It was a beautiful sunny day, with a cool breeze rustling the brightly colored fall leaves on their branches.

"Okay," Fannie said, curious. It wasn't like John to be hesitant in his conversations.

"Were you aware that the people of our community hold you and your late husband in the highest esteem?"

Fannie was confounded by his question and forgot her manners all together in her reply. "What an odd question, John."

She expected him to chuckle, but he remained very serious. "I am going somewhere with this, but I need to hear the answer before I continue."

"Okay, well I know that we both grew up here and courted and married, as expected. We had a loving marriage and six wonderful children who still adore him, even though he is gone. God is a presence in our home, and family and the community are our rock. Everyone misses Peter and so many people have been so very kind to me, sending work my way and helping us cope as we have moved on from unexpected tragedy. I call what we have in our community love, or faith, but never thought of it as esteem." She ended there, still not understanding what he could possibly be leading up to with such a question.

He gave a serious nod, and said "I met your son Peter Jr. recently."

"Okay." Fannie didn't know what else to say at that point. She was dumbfounded.

"He is such a well-spoken boy. He is going to be a good man, in spite of your family's loss." His eyes held hers as he spoke. "I just wanted you to know that."

Fannie felt tears welling in her eyes. "Why would you feel the need to say such a thing, John?"

He leaned closely into her, enough so that she could feel the heat from his body, and spoke quietly. "I just don't think that anyone has ever told you that. Peter Jr. is a hard-working, wonderful boy, and while I know, from a conversation I had with him, that his spending so much time at work, and away from home, worries you, just know that it is in an effort to ease some of your financial burden – though he would never tell you that. He confided in me while we worked at the Houghton's farm the other day, and I just needed you to hear it. He is quiet at home and school because he is tired, Fannie, not because he doesn't love you or his siblings."

Fannie had given up the attempt to not cry and let the tears flow freely down her face now. It had never occurred to her that her eldest son was working so much because he was trying to help her. And here was John, bringing her such reassurance and peace regarding his behavior. "Thank you for telling me that, John," she said quietly, leaning even a little closer toward him. "But why the question about the community holding me and Peter in the highest esteem?"

John considered her with a piercing gaze for a moment, and then took a deep breath, obviously gearing up to answer her finally. "I asked you that because I know how close you are with so many of the community members, and I have been welcomed here with open arms. But they are very protective of you and I think that sometimes they treat you with kid gloves when you don't need it."

Surprised, Fannie asked, "What makes you say that?"

"He reached out and took her hand gently in his. Well, first off, they are so worried that you will not be able to cope with the realities of what your children have been going through, that they have tried to hide certain truths. One being how much and how hard Pete Jr. has been working, and why. They have not told you about some of the troubles that your other sons have been having at school. They have not told you how your daughter, May, is still grieving most openly. Nor have they told you that your youngest has been more reserved than they would like. They have shared these truths with me, a virtual stranger, rather than with you, one of their own. And it's not out of cruelty or ill will, it is meant to protect you. But I suspect you already knew these things and more about your children's state the last year. Am I right?"

Fannie nodded. There was nothing else to do. Everything that she had heard was the truth, and the fact that the community she loved so dearly was not telling her everything was a suspicion that she had long had.

"And," John continued, gathering her other hand in his, "I don't think you are unaware of any of this, and I think that you have been fighting through it. I believe that your resolve, support and love are why the children in your life are doing as well as they are."

She blinked away the tears that were clouding her vision, but more just kept coming. She was undone by his words and wanted nothing more than to melt into the one person that really, truly understood what she was going through.

"And the other reason I ask is that, I think that when they think of you, they always think of you and Peter as one. Now that he is gone, they see you as Peter's widow, rather than the smart, driven, strong, independent woman that you are. They are waiting for you to fall apart, rather than preparing themselves for when you finally blossom into who you are meant to be in your new reality. Peter didn't hold you back, but the memory that the community has assigned him for you has been."

"John..." she spoke his name low.

"Please let me finish, Fannie." She nodded and he continued, lifting his hand to brush tears off of her cheeks. "What they don't realize is that you will thrive no matter what. And I am willing to bet that Peter knew that about you." She nodded again. "They are so very protective of you," he continued, putting his hand on her other cheek. They warned me that this project would be too big and stressful for you. I didn't listen. Just from the little that I had heard and observed, I knew you would more than handle it. And when I asked about you, they warned me away, saying you are Peter's widow. But I don't want to listen. Fannie, there is so much more life in you, and I want to be there to live it with you and your amazing children."

Stunned, all Fannie could manage was, "you asked about me?"

His face softened and he chuckled for the first time since the conversation started. "Of course I did. I would be a fool not to ask about you. And from what I have seen these past weeks, I know that all of my suspicions were correct. You are not only beautiful and talented, but you are strong, perceptive, and fiercely protective of those that you hold dear.

"John, what does all of this mean?" She had never expected such attention from John. He had maintained the boundaries or friendship so distinctly, while she was the one that had felt such a strong attraction and connection to him. She had never thought that he noticed her as more than a friendly companion. "I didn't think that you saw me that way?"

"Oh, Fannie, now that I know you and who you truly are, I could never see you any differently." And ever so gently, he pulled her close to him and rested his lips against hers. She responded in kind and they melted into each other, breathing in what each had wanted from the other for so long.

And so it was that as the hours passed into days, and the days into months, and the months into years, Fannie and John's bond grew and encompassed the children that she brought into the world with her first love and raised into adult with her second and last love. The love and admiration that they knew for each other and their family were boundless. They lived peacefully in the sanctuary that they had found sanctuary in each other – friends and lovers that knew each other better than anyone else in the world.

RECKLESSLY AMISH

SAMANTHA COLLIER

Chapter One
Loss

John puffed slightly as he walked over the plain, taking off his black hat to wipe sweat from his brow. This shouldn't be happening. Still at least twenty minutes from home. His father was going to be angry.

Well, he hadn't planned for it. When the wheel had started wobbling on the buggy as he cantered along the familiar dirt road, he had slowed down. He had done everything that he could think of to get the thing home. Yes, he knew that his father had told him to adjust it days ago, but he had just plumb forgot. And then, of course, it had completely left the axle, causing the buggy to veer off into the ditch. He didn't have anything on him to fix it. So he had left it, and started walking. The horses weren't up to bare back riding.

He knew that this was a short cut; he had heard people talking about it. Veer over the plains, rather than take the road. He was still unfamiliar with the area, but he knew enough landmarks to be okay. Well, he had no other choice. He had to get home, and quickly.

It was only supposed to be a quick trip into town, to get a few things his mother needed for the Easter dinner. They had relatives arriving for the feast, all the way from Indiana, where they had recently moved from. His parents were counting on him. And then, this had to happen.

John stopped, frowning, as he surveyed the landscape. He thought he was going the right way, but it all looked the same. With a pained sigh, he started off again. Luckily, it was a perfect spring day, not a cloud in the sky. If a trifle hot.

He set off, again. It shouldn't be too much further, surely?

And that's when he saw the figure on horseback, riding over the plain like it was being pursued by half of the state. A black horse, tall and handsome. He couldn't quite make out the rider; could just see the figure crouched over the horse, spurring it on to greater speed. Really, the person was riding the horse way too fast. Yes, it was an open plain, but John knew the hard way that there were many dips and hidden holes here. He had stepped into a couple, by accident.

If the horse stepped into one, it would lose its footing entirely, and at the speed they were going, throw the rider clean off. It would also be lucky not to break its leg, and everyone knew that was the worst thing that could happen to a horse. It would be the death of the creature.

The rider approached, still at full speed. The person could see him...surely? But it didn't slow down. Instead, it approached him with such ferocity that John instinctively dived to the left.

His hat fell off, rolling down an embankment. He got up, seething with anger. The fool had almost caused another accident. He watched as the rider reined in the horse, then turned it back toward him.

"Are you alright?" The figure atop the horse gazed down at him.

John looked up, about to give the man a piece of his mind, when the words froze on his lips. It wasn't a man. No, it was a girl, and an Amish girl, at that. Still with her prayer *kapps* on her head, although it had become slightly dislodged by the wild ride. As had her hair; instead of a neat bun, it was flowing down her back.

John gaped. He had simply never seen a girl ride like that, with no awareness of her surroundings or her appearance. Who on earth was she?

"I said, are you alright?" The girl's voice sounded impatient. Well, that took the cake. She had almost ploughed into him with her horse, and there was no apology.

John brushed off his dark pants. There were scuff marks on them; his mother was not going to be happy. He was dressed in his best clothes for the feast, not his regular work ones. This day was just getting worse.

"No thanks to you," John spat, glaring up at the girl. "What do you think you were doing, riding the horse so fast towards me?"

The girl had the gall to laugh, throwing her head back so that her hair fell down her back.

"I thought you would move," she said, her eyes glittering. "Don't worry, you were never in any danger. I've been riding horses since I could walk."

"Well, then, you should know that riding one that fast on a pock holed plain is a bad idea," John answered, sourly. He waited for the apology that was his due. But she simply looked at him, smiling bemusedly.

"Who are you?" she asked, cocking her head to the side as she assessed him. "I've never seen you before."

"John Miller," he said, stiffly. "My family has only just moved here, a month ago."

"Are you living at the old Yoder farmhouse?"

"*Jah.*" He scratched his head, looking up at her. "That's where I am heading, now. The wheel came off my buggy on the road, and I was told this was a shortcut."

"A shortcut to where?" She laughed, again. "You are heading in the wrong direction. You need to go that way." She pointed west. He looked, confused. He was sure he had been going the right way.

"Well, John Miller," she laughed, grabbing the reins, "good luck!" She took off at high speed, flying back over the plain in the opposite direction.

He watched her, his jaw open, riding like the wind until she was a mere speck on the horizon.

John picked up his hat, dusty on the ground. Who on earth was she? He had never known an Amish girl to be quite so.... reckless. He was used to demure and apologetic girls, who would never ride alone, and certainly not in the way that she had. Maybe the Amish girls were different in this part of the country? He hadn't really spoken to any, not yet. His family had attended a few church services, but he hadn't really socialised. He thought of Miriam, the girl he had been sweet on back in Indiana. Miriam would never have dreamt of riding like that, and would certainly have never spoken the way that the girl had.

He eventually got to the farmhouse, his mood sour. The family were all assembled at the table, waiting for him. His father stood up, frowning, watching his son walk through the door.

"Where have you been, John?" The older man's jaw tightened.

"It is a long story," John sighed. "The wheel came off the buggy, and I had to walk over the plain. Then I almost got knocked over by a horse. A girl on a black horse, riding like the wind." He shook his head, not believing his own words.

His mother had got to her feet. "You look a mess," she said. "Go and clean up." She sat back down. "Did you say a girl on a black horse? I have heard of her. The church elders of the district have talked of her, and not in a good way."

"What is her name?" John asked. He could still picture her in his mind's eye, hair flowing, eyes glittering.

"Sarah Glick?" His mother frowned, trying to remember. "*Jah*, I am sure that is her name. She is a wild one, that is for sure. You were lucky to walk away from her unscathed by the sound of it, John."

Sarah. The wild girl, who rode like a man. Well, he would make sure that he had nothing to do with her, ever again. A girl needed to be demure, and she didn't seem to know the meaning of the word.

As John walked off to the bathroom to wash, he tried to dislodge the vision of her from his mind. But she stayed with him, all through the lunch, and the tedious rest of the day, going back to fix the buggy, his father haranguing him the whole way.

***

Sarah dismounted Racer, giving the sweating black horse a kiss on his nose. "Thank you," she whispered. "That was a wonderful ride."

She waked into the house, tossing off her *kapps* as she went. Where was Mamm?

Right at that moment, her mother walked out of the kitchen, wiping flour on her apron. She stopped short when she saw her daughter, frowning.

"Sarah," she said, through gritted teeth, "where is your *kapps*? And your hair! It has come completely undone."

Sarah laughed. "It is always does," she said, nonchalantly. "The silly *kapps* can't contain it."

"Have you been riding too fast again?" Her mother had her hands on her hips as she looked at her.

Sarah's eyes flashed. "Why do you have to keep harping on about it?" she said, her voice raised. "I like to ride fast! And so does Racer."

"Sarah, it isn't seemly..."

Sarah rounded on her mother. "Why?" she shouted. "I have been hearing this forever! Who says that just because I am a girl I can't ride fast?"

Her mother sighed, closing her eyes. "We have talked about it many times," she said. "A girl in our community has to be meek, or at least not as wild as you are. You want to stay in our community, don't you?"

"*Jah*," admitted Sarah, breathing heavily. "You know that I do! I just can't understand why I can't be myself. Why are there all these silly rules and regulations? Why can a boy do what he likes but a girl can't?"

Her mother sighed, again. "It is just the way it is," she whispered. "It has always been that way. If you choose to be in our community, you must be respectful. People already gossip about you too much. It hurts your father, and myself."

Sarah rolled her eyes. "Small minded people," she spat. "Why do you care what they say?" She turned away, walking to the stairs. "I have to change."

Her mother watched her walk away, in despair. "Sarah," she called. "Rebecca needs you to mind the children, tomorrow."

Sarah's hand tightened on the balustrade. Not again. She really didn't enjoy looking after her sister's children. Oh, it might get better when they were older, and she could talk to them, and they could answer back. Have a conversation. She loved her niece and nephew, but babies bored her. So much mess and crying. Sarah preferred older children, who could come riding and skating with her.

"Do I have to?" she sighed, looking back at her mother.

"*Jah*," her mother answered. "You really do. I must finish my quilts for the sale, and Katie is busy, as well. It won't be for long, but you will have to get there early."

"Alright." Sarah continued up the stairs, not looking back again. Her mother watched her for a moment, then sighed heavily and went back into the kitchen.

Sarah collapsed across her bed. Another tedious day of child minding, when all she wanted to do was ride. It was such lovely weather; there was nothing she loved more in the world, than racing across the plains on Racer. He enjoyed it, too. Tomorrow was supposed to be wonderful, and now she would be cooped up inside her sister's house, trying to entertain a nine-month-old and a toddler.

Suddenly, the vision of the man on the plain today flashed through her mind. John Miller. He had looked at her like she was something from another world. Disapproving, as everyone was; Sarah had seen the sour look on his face. It was disappointing. She had thought that because he was new to the district, he might have an open mind. But all he saw was a girl on a horse, riding too fast, with a crooked prayer *kapps* and dislodged hair.

A pity. He was very handsome. Tall, with dark hair. Intriguing. Sarah mulled the vision of him over in her mind.

***

"Sarah, make sure you get into those corners," her mother said, depositing the bucket and mop at her feet. Then she walked out of the kitchen.

Sarah sighed dramatically, staring at the bucket. Tedious chores, before the day had even begun. Not that there was much to look forward to, anyway. Just babysitting.

She put the mop into the bucket, then slopped water on the floor, spreading it around disinterestedly. She didn't care what her mother said; there was no way she was moving stuff around. A quick going over with it, and then she was out of here.

Sarah hated housework, even more than babysitting, and that was saying something. Why couldn't she just be free to ride all day, the wind in her face, feeling the ground thunder beneath Racer's hooves?

At last. Mopping done, Sarah rushed out of the house, heading toward the stables. He would be getting restless. He always enjoyed a morning talk, even if she wasn't able to ride out. Racer. He had been her horse since she was twelve years old, and she liked him better than anyone.

She saddled him up, talking to him as she did so. "Not a long ride today, Racer," she said. "More's the pity. We have to head to Rebecca's to look after the babies." Racer looked at her with his deep brown eyes, seeming to sense the sorrow in her. He nudged her gently.

She was just about to head out, when her mother stopped her. "I don't want to hear any reports from people about you," she said, looking up at Sarah in the saddle. "No wild rides. Straight to your sister's house, young lady."

Sarah rolled her eyes. "Of course," she said. She picked up the reins, spurring Racer out of the stable.

It was a beautiful day, just as she had known it would be. Wildflowers bloomed everywhere; the trees swayed in the distance. Sarah stopped, breathing in the scent. She just felt more alive, somehow, out in nature. It was unnatural to be cooped up inside, tending babies and doing eternal housework. How did most women deal with it, after they were married?

She would never marry, she decided suddenly. At least, then, she wouldn't have to be a slave to a man and the children that would inevitably come. But the alternative didn't really appeal to her, either: being a spinster maid, living with her parents forever, at her mother's beck and call. What to do?

She wouldn't think about it, at all. She would just enjoy the ride. She spurred Racer on, heading across the plains towards her sister's farmhouse.

The wind felt so good. Surely one little ride, where she let Racer stretch his legs, couldn't hurt? She would still be able to get to Rebecca's on time.

Decision made, she spurred him on, flying across the plain. Freedom. A wide smile spread across her face, lodging there. There was no better feeling in the world.

The world whizzed past her, blurring. Racer picked up speed.

Suddenly, he stopped, rearing up. What was it? She barely had time to see the snake, as she flew over the horse's head, landing with a thud on the ground.

She sat up, slowly. The world was spinning. Had she knocked her head? She tried to get up, but it was all too much. She had to sit back down again.

"Are you alright?"

She jumped, almost leaping out of her skin. A figure in black loomed over her. She squinted, trying to make out who it was. Where on earth had they materialised from? She hadn't seen anyone on the plain, not even in the distance.

Then, she knew. She remembered. It was the man she had seen yesterday, John Miller.

"*Jah*, I think so," she said ruefully, rubbing her head. "I don't know what happened."

"A snake is what happened," John said. "I saw it as I was running over to you."

"A snake?" Sarah wrinkled up her nose. "But it's too early for them."

"It's because of the warm weather we've been having," he said. "They come out earlier." He crouched down, looking at her. "You were very lucky. I saw you go clear over your horse's head. Have you any injuries?"

Sarah tried to concentrate on his voice. But the sight of him, crouching down close to her, made her catch her breath. She had been right. He was a very handsome man, and she was enjoying the look of concern that was in his face as he stared at her.

"I think so," she said, gingerly. Maybe he would carry her in his arms? The thought made her glow, for a moment. Then she shook her head at her own muddled thinking.

"Try to stand up," he said. She did so, feeling woozy. But at least she was on her feet, which was something.

"Where were you going?" John asked now, reaching out to steady her. The touch of his hand on hers made her heart thump. What on earth was happening to her? It must be because of the fall. It had addled her wits, temporarily.

"To my sister's," she answered. It seemed so long ago that she had set out for Rebecca's. Was she late? That was all she needed. Rebecca would complain to their mother, and she would never hear the end of it.

"Do you want me to help you get there?" he asked, frowning. "Or do you want to go home?"

Sarah grimaced. If she headed home, her mother would scold her all day about her recklessness. No, better to push on to Rebecca's. At least, then, she could salvage the situation. A little.

"I need to get there," she said, starting to walk. She turned back to look at him. "Why are you out here?"

He blushed, slightly. Why, she didn't know. "I was just going for a walk," he said, slowly. Why wouldn't he meet her eyes? It was like he wasn't telling her the truth. But why would that be? She shook her head, slightly. She was being fanciful, again.

She went up to Racer, grabbing his reins, talking to him soothingly. Then she put her foot in the stirrup.

"What are you doing?" John approached her quickly. "You can't ride. You've had a nasty fall. I will walk with you. We can lead the horse."

Sarah turned to him, astonished. "But I will be late," she said, gritting her teeth. "And I am perfectly fine!"

"Why are you so stubborn?" he said, frowning at her. "Your sister will understand why you are late when we explain it to her."

Sarah shook her head. She was appalled to find tears had sprung into her eyes. "You don't understand," she said, bitterly. "She will know why I fell, and so why I am late, and then she will start scolding me, as everyone does!" A single tear fell down on her cheek. Oh, this was so frustrating! She wasn't one of those girls who cried at the drop of a hat. She rarely cried over anything. Why then, did she feel as if she were about start sobbing like silly Grace Fisher, the cry baby back at school?

John leant over, stroking her arm. She looked up at him, appalled to see sympathy in his eyes. Yes, he was feeling sorry for her. He must think she was like all the other girls he had ever met.

"Sarah, it's alright," he said, soothingly.

"How do you know my name?" she said, sniffling. "I never told you yesterday."

John started. "I told my family about you, when I eventually got home," he said, carefully.

Sarah's eyes widened. "Oh, I see," she said, in a disappointed voice. "Of course. Everyone has heard of me, even people who are new to the district. Silly Sarah Glick, who rides her horse too fast, dislikes babies and hates housework."

John smiled. "Well, I didn't know you hated housework," he said. He stared at her, his eyes glowing. Sarah felt her breath stop, again.

"Why does everyone disapprove of me?" she burst out, gazing at John. As if she expected an answer! He would just start lecturing her, the same as everyone else. He had done so, yesterday. She was so used to it she barely noticed it anymore.

"I suppose," he said, slowly, "because you are different to the other girls in our faith. People want everyone to be the same, and feel the same."

Sarah gasped. "*Jah*," she breathed. "That is so true!" She felt sorry for herself. She was a duckling in a swan's nest, there was no doubt about it. Did this John understand that? He seemed to.

"I think you are wonderful," he blurted, gazing at her. "But you should be careful with your riding. I would hate to see you get hurt."

"You think I am wonderful?" Sarah breathed. She gazed at him. Maybe he wasn't like all the others.

But then, he had told her to be careful, as well. And was that a slight frown on his face?

"You can escort me to my sisters," she said, stiffly. "Thank you for coming to my service. I appreciate it."

She started walking off, leading Racer.

She didn't see the look of longing that John Miller gave her, as he slowly followed her.

***

Her sister was down the steps of her veranda as soon as they arrived.

"Sarah! Where on earth have you been? You are over an hour late!" Rebecca had her hands on her hips, frowning.

Sarah shrugged. "I fell off Racer," she said. "John helped me."

"You fell off Racer?" Rebecca repeated. "Are you hurt?"

Sarah shrugged, again. "I feel well, I think," she said. She handed Racer's reins to John. "Would you be able to take him to the stable for me? It's just around the back."

"Certainly," said John, taking the reins. He looked at her for a moment, then led the horse away.

Rebecca gazed after him. "Who is he?" she whispered. "I don't think I have ever seen him before."

"His name is John Miller," answered Sarah. "He has just moved here with his family."

Rebecca gazed at her, her eyes wide. "And he just happened along, after your fall?"

"*Jah*," Sarah said. "He was out walking. I bumped into him yesterday, as well."

They started walking up the farmhouse steps. "I think that young man likes you, Sarah," Rebecca whispered.

Sarah stopped. "What are you talking about? He just happened along, and was nice enough to assist me."

Rebecca smiled. "I can tell, by the way he looks at you," she said. She narrowed her eyes, looking over her sister. "It's good that you look decent today, even though you had a fall. I have seen you with your hair out, and your *kapps* dislodged. Dirt on your apron. At least you are looking better than usual."

Sarah felt stung. "You are too concerned with appearances, sister," she said, primly. "And as for any interest from that young man, you are imagining it. Besides, I never want to court anyone. I don't want to marry, and get stuck in a farmhouse being a slave, tending to screaming babies forever."

Rebecca looked at her as if she had lost her mind. "There is more to it than that, little sister," she said sharply. "What about love – for your husband, and your children? To serve those you love is a blessing. I couldn't imagine life without my family."

"I'm not criticising you..."

"Enough." Rebecca put a hand in the air to silence her. "You are young, and foolish. I hope that you will see the error of your ways before it is too late, Sarah. For you just might find life passes you by, and suddenly you are a spinster dreaming of what could have been." She walked ahead into the house.

Sarah frowned. Rebecca was just justifying her choices, wasn't she? Not that there were many, really. If you belonged to the community, you always ended up being a wife and mother. Love. Sarah scoffed. Was so called love worth all the nonsense attached to it? Nothing had led her to believe so, thus far.

And yet. She remembered how she had felt, when John had helped her up. The fission of attraction. But what did it matter, anyway? John would prove himself like all the rest of them. Wanting to change her.

Here he was, now. Walking toward her. Her heart started beating faster.

"Sarah." He bowed, his dark eyes shining. She looked at him, awkwardly. What should she say? Should she invite him inside, for a drink? It would probably be polite. After all, he had helped her today.

"Would you like a glass of water, or a coffee?" She blushed, slightly.

"No, no," he said. "I should get going. Chores to do." And yet he stood there, still looking at her.

"Well," Sarah looked at the ground. "Thank you for helping me today. I really appreciated it."

"My pleasure," he said. He looked at her, almost beseechingly. Then he abruptly turned on his heel, and walked away. Back up the track.

Sarah watched him go. She was feeling odd. Was John Miller a friend, or a critic? Was she being judged by him?

She simply didn't know. She only knew that she wanted him to come back. To be by her side. For just a little bit longer.

***

John walked briskly. He was going to be in trouble with his father, again. He didn't even know why he had decided to walk across the plain this morning. He had many chores to do, and his father knew how long each one took. He would be at the farm, now, wondering where on earth John had disappeared to.

He frowned. He was only being half truthful with himself. He knew why he had suddenly decided on the morning walk. He had been hoping to see Sarah again.

He hadn't been able to stop thinking about her. It was as simple as that. He knew that she was considered wild by the community. He knew everyone thought that she wasn't marriage material, that she was too forthright, and reckless. He had seen the evidence of that recklessness, not once, but twice. Yesterday, when she had almost run him down with her horse. And today, when she had fallen from it.

He thought her reckless, like everybody else. And yet, there was something so charismatic about her. The vision of the girl on the horse, hair flying and eyes glittering, was enchanting. And the fact that she had the strength of will to be herself, in the face of disapproval.

But she had admitted it, today. She hated housework, and didn't like babies. How could he sensibly try to court a young woman who had no desire to set up a home and have a family, as was the done thing in their faith? John was a conventional man. He wanted a home and family of his own; he wanted to have children. How could he court a girl who expressed her disdain for both?

He thought of Miriam, the girl he had been courting. Meek Miriam, whose sole desire in life was marriage and children. She was the type of woman he should be considering, not a wild girl like Sarah who flouted convention.

He sighed, deeply. He had better get moving. Sarah would probably not agree to courting him, anyway, with her beliefs. If he suggested it to her, she would probably laugh in his face.

Best to forget all about her. With a nod of decision, John set off towards his farm.

***

The babies were screaming. Sarah had a thudding headache. She didn't know if it was a leftover from her fall today, or just the children. Maybe a combination of both.

Would they ever stop? She had tried everything. Fed them, changed them, tried to get them to sleep. But still, they carried on. She juggled little Eli, the nine-month-old, on her hip, desperately looking down the track to see if Rebecca's buggy was on the way. Samuel, the toddler, had his arms wrapped around her legs, bawling like a banshee.

"Your Mamm will be home soon," she said, in a false cheery voice. "Let's sit on the sofa with a picture book."

She walked into the living room, picking up a book. It was one of her own favorites from childhood. She settled down on the sofa, getting Samuel to crawl up beside her. She kept Eli on her lap.

It was difficult, juggling the book and the baby, but she managed to get it open. And then she started reading.

It was such a sweet story, and she got lost in it, just a little bit. The children quietened down as she read. She could feel Eli's head starting to loll. Samuel snuggled up closer, his eyes riveted onto the book.

As she read the last page, she was amazed to see that Eli had fallen asleep. And Samuel was almost there. He burrowed his head into her side, kissing her.

Her heart melted, just a little bit. She looked at him, being very careful that she didn't disturb Eli.

"Did you like that story, little one?" she whispered. Samuel looked up at her, his big blue eyes shining. He nodded.

"Sa-rah," he said, stringing out her name, as he always did. "I love you."

Sarah gasped. He had never said those words to her, before.

"I love you, too, Samuel," she whispered, leaning over to kiss him on the head. He sighed contentedly, before his eyelids started fluttering and finally closed. He was asleep.

Sarah closed the book. It hadn't been easy, but she had got there. They had settled down. Reading the book had been the trick. Even when they had kept crying, she had continued. Her calm determination had soothed them.

Was that the trick, with babies? Being calm? Not getting upset when they cried?

She knew in her heart that it wasn't always that simple. She had seen Rebecca, the calmest person she knew, sometimes unable to settle them. But it did seem to help. And it made her feel better able to cope with them, if she was feeling calm, instead of stressed and anxious.

And how sweet that moment had been, when little Samuel had told her he loved her.

The front door opened. It was Caleb, Rebecca's husband. She looked at him, raising a finger to her mouth to signal to be quiet. Caleb smiled, walking quietly into the living room.

"Well, well," he whispered. "What do we have here? Well done, Sarah."

Sarah glowed. Usually, whenever Caleb walked into the house when she was looking after the children, it was bedlam. He would have to take over, settling the babies, and Sarah, frazzled, would look for her escape.

They both turned as they heard the buggy pull up outside. And then, Rebecca walked into the room. She raised her eyebrows in amazement at the calm scene in front of her.

"Sarah," she whispered. "What has happened? Where is my hot headed little sister?"

Sarah smiled. Rebecca gently eased Eli out of her arms, carrying him to his cot. Caleb did the same with Samuel, making cooing sounds to the little boy as he stirred in his arms.

Sarah watched her sister and brother-in-law meet in the hallway, after putting their children down. Caleb rested a hand on Rebecca's arm, and she gazed up at him with such a look of love that Sarah gasped.

She had to turn her head away from the tender scene, blinking back tears. Why was she so overcome with emotion? It was inexplicable.

As she said good bye to them, she couldn't resist poking her head into the children's bedrooms, watching them sleep. They looked so precious. Her heart overflowed with love for them.

She rode Racer over the plain, heading home. For once, she listened to the voice in her head that said to not go too fast. She didn't feel the need. And she was half hoping that she might spot John Miller, walking.

But she didn't see him. Why did she feel so disappointed? She barely knew the man, after all.

And he would never deign to court her. Her reputation preceded her, and he was a solemn man. Even though his eyes shone when he beheld her. Sarah shivered, picturing them in her mind.

John's dark eyes followed her all the way home, over the plain.

***

A week passed. Sarah rode out over the plain, but she didn't see him. She tried to tell herself it was for the best. She told herself that he was too solemn for her; they wouldn't have been a good match.

But still, her heart yearned to see him. Her heart would jump when she would see a figure in the distance, her eyes deceiving her. It was him! But it never was. He had obviously decided that she was too hard work.

Today was a magical spring day, a hint of summer in the air. She had ridden Racer a bit, but not too fast. Maybe her fall had made her more cautious, she had no idea. But suddenly, she was aware that her beloved horse could be injured by her recklessness. It just didn't seem worth it, anymore.

She bent down to pick some wildflowers. She thought of the bible passage that she had read last night. It had made her stop and ponder. It was Proverbs 14:16, which said, "One who is wise is cautious and turns away from evil, but a fool is reckless and careless." Had that been her? Had she smashed through life, careless of what was before her? She didn't think that she was a fool. She wanted to be wise.

Suddenly, she looked up. Was it really him, on the horizon? John Miller? Her heart started thumping, uncomfortably.

It was. He walked slowly toward her, his face solemn. And then, he was standing there.

"I thought it was you," he said, his eyes shining. He looked down at the ground, as if he didn't know what to say further.

"John," Sarah said, staring at him. She took a deep breath. It was now, or never.

"*Jah*?" He looked up at her. His face told her all she needed to know.

"I'm sorry," she whispered. "I realise now that I have been reckless. I want to change."

"What?" He looked like he couldn't believe what she had just said.

"Oh, I will probably never be meek," she admitted. "I have a temper. But I have learnt that I should try to control it, and remain calm. I want to be a better person."

He looked at her in amazement. "Sarah," he said. "I love you. For who you are. I wouldn't want you to change. I like that you are different from the other girls." He blushed. "Maybe just tone it down, a little."

"You love me?" she whispered. Her heart overflowed with gladness. "John, I love you, too!"

He stared at her, as if he had never heard such good news. He gently approached her. She gazed up at him, her heart overflowing.

"So, I may court you?" he whispered. "And one day we might marry? Even though you hate housework and don't like babies?"

She laughed, gently. "I mightn't ever like housework," she admitted. "But I know it is a necessary part of life. As for babies – well, maybe one day?" She looked at him, blushing.

He smiled. "Maybe one day," he said. "We can have a long engagement, and wait until you feel you are ready. I don't mind waiting."

Sarah breathed a sigh of relief, and gratitude. It was simply astonishing. A man who was willing to give her the space she needed, and loved her for herself, despite her faults. Who was willing to not listen to everything that he had heard, but simply judge her on what he saw.

That was a man worth keeping. She finally understood what this love thing was all about.

THE END

AMISH HIDEAWAY

STEPHANIE SWIFT

Anna Brenneman hummed softly and smiled as she scribbled homework instructions on the blackboard. It was finally Friday. Only three more weeks remained of the school year term, and that fact was more than evident by her student's behavior. Everyone was excited and anxious for the term to come to an end, and that resulted in less concentration on schoolwork and more attention on talking about summer plans. Not that she could blame them because she was ready for a much-needed break too.

"Okay, class…Monday we'll be working on the last group project before your final exams, so I need everyone to divide up into groups of four," she said.

It didn't take much prompting for the children to jump from their seats and gravitate to their best friends. As usual, the boys stuck together in their little cliques, and so did the girls, but Anna noticed one student, eight-year-old Hope Roth, still sitting at her desk, busily drawing something on a piece of paper. She seemed oblivious to everything happening around her.

"Hope?" she called.

Still no reaction.

"Okay, everyone, I want you to move your desks into a circle pattern with your group, so you can work together on ideas for your project. Try to do it quietly!"

As the others did as they were told, Anna walked over to Hope's desk and knelt beside it.

"Hope, sweetie, what are you doing?" she asked.

She glanced at Hope's paper and discovered she'd drawn a photo of a table with a tall pitcher of lemonade and glasses sitting on top of it, and "Lemonade: 25 cents" was scrawled in huge letters at the top of the page.

"My *daed* is going to build a stand for me like this one so I can sell lemonade this summer and make some money for us."

Anna cringed. Why would any adult ask a eight-year-old to take on a job, even something as small as selling lemonade at a roadside stand? She knew that Hope and her father had fallen on some hard times in the wake of her mother's passing from cancer many months prior, but she had no idea it had gotten so bad.

"That's nice, Hope, but I need you to put your colors away so you can focus on the project we're working on for next week. Will you do that for me?"

Hope hung her head and pursed her lips.

"Do I have to, Miss Brenneman? I'd rather work on my lemonade business."

It sounded so strange and very sad hearing grown-up words coming from such a small child. Part of her wanted to let her forego the project because her "business" seemed so important to her, but she knew it wouldn't be fair to the other children if she showed favoritism. After much persuading, she managed to talk Hope into joining three other girls in the classroom who needed one more participant to form their group, but she didn't seem happy about it at all.

Her heart ached as she watched Hope lay her head down on her desk and half-heartedly listen to the other girls plan the outline for their project. It bothered her greatly when any of her students were hurting, but knowing the sadness Hope had endured since her mother's death made her situation even more disconcerting.

Anna made a mental note to speak to her father about it when he picked her up after school, but at the end of the day, while she was busy putting away her classroom supplies, Anna glanced out one of the school building windows and noticed Hope walking the dirt road home with Ivy and Leah, two other classmates.

Anna walked outside where a couple of the other children were waiting to be picked up. She saw a horse-drawn wagon approaching from the opposite direction, but it wasn't being driven by Hope's father.

"Thomas, have you seen Mr. Caleb Roth?"

The young boy, who was close in age to Hope, shrugged his shoulders. "Hope said he must have forgotten, so she decided to walk home with Ivy and Leah."

He said it so nonchalantly, as if Hope's father forgetting to pick up his daughter from school was no big deal, but it made Anna angry. Who forgets to pick up their child from school? She tried to rationalize it. Perhaps something happened to delay him. The thought made her pulse race, and she prayed he wasn't hurt. Hope was already struggling with losing her mother. Losing both her parents would be devastating.

Anna tried to push the troubling thought from her mind. It was probably something unavoidable that couldn't be helped, and there was no reason to jump to conclusions or think the worst. Still, as she returned to her classroom and continued putting things away, she couldn't shake the gnawing feeling that something wasn't right.

* * * *

Caleb Roth pulled on the reins and brought his plow horse to a stop when a bright glimmer in the distance caught his attention. Shielding his eyes from the sun with his hand, he tried to locate where the glare was coming from, and his heart dropped to his feet when he spotted his daughter, Hope, walking the dirt road toward their house. The sun danced off her metal lunch pail, and he groaned and hung his head in shame.

He'd forgotten again.

It was the second time in the past two months he'd forgotten to pick Hope up from school, and he felt like kicking himself. Caleb dropped the reins and walked over to the wooden fence lining the pasture to greet her. When she caught sight of him, she took off running in his direction, her long blonde braid bouncing behind her and a smile lighting up her angelic little face.

Caleb sighed. She looked so much like her mother when she smiled, with their matching dimples and big, soulful brown eyes. As much as he loved her taking after Abigail, he couldn't deny that there were moments when the similarities gripped his heart and squeezed like a vise. When she got to the fence, she put her schoolbooks and lunch pail on the ground and climbed the fence so she could hug him.

"I'm so sorry I forgot to pick you up from school. I started plowing, and I just lost track of time. Can you forgive me?"

She gave him a curious look and giggled, as if he'd just said the funniest thing.

"Of course, I can," she said. "It's okay. I had fun walking with Ivy and Leah. Did you know that Ivy's sister, Clara, is getting married next month? Their mom is making her dress, and I bet it's going to be beautiful!"

He smiled at her comment, although a part of him ached when he considered the many things she would miss out on as she got older, including Abigail designing her own wedding dress. He knew God had a reason for taking her so soon, but he still didn't understand it and probably never would.

"Oh! I drew something for you today," she exclaimed.

She jumped off the fence long enough to retrieve a piece of paper from one of her school books.

"Can you build this for me, *daed*? I want to sell lemonade this summer, and Leah said I could probably put it on the sidewalk outside her mom's quilt shop in town, if that's okay with you."

He unfolded the piece of paper, and his heart melted when he saw the colored wooden stand and several stick figure people holding glasses of lemonade. She also drew a likeness of her behind the stand, complete with brown eyes and a long braid in her blonde hair.

"I'm sure I can probably come up with something that will work," he replied.

Hope clapped her hands together excitedly and leaned over the fence so she could kiss his cheek.

"Why don't you go clean up and do your homework while I finish up here? I'll check it when I come inside, and we'll get started on dinner, so we can discuss this lemonade stand of yours."

She nodded and smiled before picking up her supplies and running toward the house. Caleb looked at the drawing one more time before folding it up neatly and putting it inside his shirt pocket.

"She's got your eye for business, Abigail," he said softly, as he looked up at the blue sky and rolling clouds. "I know you'd be proud."

* * * *

Anna tapped her fingers against her knee as she and Hope sat on the front steps outside the schoolhouse the following afternoon. Thirty minutes had passed and all the other children had gone home, but Hope's father still hadn't shown. Anna felt her temper steadily rise as she watched Hope aimlessly sift through one of her textbooks.

"Okay, this is ridiculous," she stated. "Come on, Hope. I'm taking you home."

Thankfully, Hope didn't put up a fuss, and in no time at all, they were tucked away inside Anna's horse-drawn buggy and heading for the Roth homestead. Anna tried to keep her anger at bay, but there was no justifiable reason for any parent to forget their child, and someone needed to speak up on Hope's behalf.

She went over the conversation in her mind repeatedly, trying to figure out a way to approach the subject gracefully, but there was no use. She was upset and Caleb Roth was going to find out soon enough just what she thought about his parenting skills, or lack thereof.

When she steered the horse and buggy into Hope's driveway ten minutes later, she caught sight of him plowing the pasture behind their home. As soon as he saw them, he stopped what he was doing and walked over to greet them. Besides the casual "hello" at church, and the wave he sometimes gave her when he did decide to pick Hope up from school, they'd never formally spoken to each other.

As he drew closer, she couldn't help but notice his unkempt wavy brown hair and the dust that littered his clothes. His long-sleeved shirt was unbuttoned at the wrists and rolled to the elbows, and the top two buttons of his shirt were undone, revealing a thin sheen of perspiration on his chest. For some reason, the messiness in his physical appearance worked together to create something very rugged and masculine, and Anna caught herself staring. Shaking her head to clear her thoughts, she tried to avert her attention elsewhere.

"Miss Brenneman, I'm truly sorry. I had a problem with my plow earlier, and once I got it repaired and started plowing, I forgot the time. Thank you so much for bringing Hope home. It won't happen again. I give you my word."

Hope dropped the reins and laced her hands on top of her lap. She had no choice but to look at him, and when she gazed into his mesmerizing green eyes, she almost tripped over her own tongue.

"Mr. Roth, I need to speak to you...alone."

Something in the tone of her voice must have caught him off guard, because he gave her a skeptical look before motioning to Hope to wait for him inside the house. When she did as he asked, he stuffed the handkerchief he was holding inside his pants pocket and crossed his arms over his chest.

"Is there something you would like to say to me, Miss Brenneman?"

She did her best to remain calm by reminding herself that he was the parent of one of her students, and she shouldn't cause trouble, but the condescending expression on his face changed that in a heartbeat. He looked like he might even start laughing, which infuriated her even more.

"Mr. Roth..."

He shook his head. "Please call me Caleb."

Anna cleared her throat. "Fine," she began again. "*Caleb*, I understand that you and Hope have had a difficult year since your wife's passing, and I am sincerely sorry for your loss, but Hope already deals with enough worries without having to wonder every day if her father is going to pick her up from school or not."

He uncrossed his arms and pressed a hand against the side of her buggy to prop himself up.

"Excuse me? What other worries do you *think* Hope has...not that losing her mother isn't enough?"

He squinted his eyes, and she could tell by the tempered sound of his voice that he was probably trying to maintain his composure, but she was past the point of caring. Hope stood and descended the steps of her buggy. When Caleb attempted to help her, she pushed his hand away. When they were standing face to face, she was suddenly struck with how tall and broad-shouldered he was, but she wasn't about to cower in front of him. If David could stand against Goliath, then she could do the same with Caleb Roth.

"As if you don't know?" she asked. "What parent asks their eight-year-old child to work all summer selling lemonade to help pay the family bills? Do you really think that's appropriate?"

Caleb took a step back, and he genuinely looked surprised by her comment because he didn't say anything for the longest while. When he did speak, his voice was much softer and calmer. His shoulders slumped and he seemed almost sad...defeated even.

"Miss Brenneman, I can assure you that I've never asked Hope to work to support us. I manage that fine on my own. She did ask me yesterday if I would build her a stand so she could sell lemonade in town this summer, but I thought she wanted to earn a little extra money to buy something new for herself."

Anna wasn't sure how to reply. She didn't know the man personally, but she could usually tell when someone was lying to her, and he wasn't lying.

"Perhaps you should get the whole story before you start passing judgement on me or anyone else for that matter," he remarked.

She probably should have apologized, but he stood up straight again and towered over her, which bristled her nerves. They were standing so close she could barely breathe.

"Have you ever lost someone close to you, Miss Brenneman?"

She put her hands on her hips and held her chin high. "No, I haven't, but I don't see what that has to do with any of this."

He continued glaring a hole straight through her, but she refused to back down.

"Since my wife died, I've been trying very hard to run our home as smoothly as she once did, but that isn't easy. I get up an hour early each morning so I can cook Hope breakfast before I take her to school. I spend the rest of the day dividing my time between washing our clothes and tending to other household chores and getting my work done on our farm so I can afford to put food on our table and pay the bills. My wife always did such a wonderful job making our house a home, and somehow she even managed to have her own vegetable garden in our backyard too, and she would tend to it daily and sell her crops to clients in town."

His speech was so impassioned, she didn't dare interrupt, not that he would have given her the opportunity.

"Every night I cook our dinner before helping Hope with her homework. When she goes to sleep, I clean the kitchen and mend any clothes that need mending. I usually go to sleep around midnight. I don't mind doing any of this though because I'm her father, and I love her more than life itself, and it's my responsibility to take care of her. Still, it's not easy, and unless you've been in my shoes, then I politely ask you to stop judging me. God Almighty is my only judge – not you."

By the time he finished speaking, he was standing so close their bodies were almost touching, and he was looking down on her with fire in his eyes and his breathing was labored. She thought about what he said, and she hated to admit that he was right. She'd never been married – or in love, for that matter. It was easy to see the depth of his love for his late wife by the way he talked about her, and she couldn't help but wonder what that must feel like – to love someone with such passion and heartfelt emotion.

Her plan to teach Caleb a lesson had backfired on her, and she felt ashamed and full of remorse. Hot tears sprang to her eyes, and she knew it would be best to retreat before she started crying – something she *did not* want him to witness.

Anna adjusted the bonnet on her head and flattened the apron on her long dress before attempting to speak.

"You're right, Caleb, and I apologize for misjudging you. It won't happen again."

She tried to ascend the steps on her buggy, but he reached out and stopped her by lightly grasping her arm.

"Anna..."

His voice was soft and soothing and the heat from his touch seared through the fabric of her dress and warmed her blood. Still, she refused to look at him, and when she jerked her arm from his grasp, he didn't try to dissuade her from leaving. Anna took her place behind the reins and steered the horse and buggy onto the main dirt road. Once she was finally out of view of Caleb, she let her tears fall where they may.

* * * *

Caleb sat at the kitchen table the next morning, mindlessly turning his coffee mug around and around on top of the wooden table...and trying not to think about Anna Brenneman.

He groaned.

It was pointless. He hadn't been able to sleep all night because every time he closed his eyes he would picture her standing in front of him with tears in her beautiful blue eyes after he berated her for insinuating he was a bad father.

He felt horrible for hurting her feelings. He knew she was just worried over her student, like any good teacher would be. After discovering the real reason Hope wanted him to build a lemonade stand, he felt as if someone had kicked him in the gut, and even though he knew he was just defending himself, he still could have been a gentleman and handled his answers with more tact.

Had he really made Hope feel like she needed a job to help support the two of them? Was he failing her somehow? The thought that he might be disappointing her in some way made his heart ache. She'd already been through so much since losing Abigail. He would never dream of putting her through anymore sorrow.

"*Daed*?"

Caleb turned to find Hope entering the kitchen, rubbing her eyes and shuffling her feet on the floor as she walked.

"Is it time for breakfast?" she asked before stifling a yawn.

Caleb stretched out his arms and she walked over to join him and climbed on top of his lap. When she rested her head on his shoulder, he kissed her forehead and rocked her back and forth, the way he used to when she was a baby.

"Not yet, sweetheart. What are you doing up so early? You still have another couple of hours before you have to get ready for school."

She yawned again. "I saw the light from the lantern, and I wanted to make sure you were okay."

He squeezed her tight.

"You worry too much about me. I'm fine."

She smiled. "That's what I'm supposed to do."

Caleb chuckled at her remark. "No, you should be focusing on what all eight-year-old girls love doing, like playing with your friends and your dolls. I don't want you to ever think that it's your job to take care of me. Miss Brenneman told me you want to sell lemonade this summer to make money for us, and you don't have to do that because I've got that under control. Any money you make will go towards buying something *you* want. Okay?"

She nodded and wrapped her little arms around his neck and held on tight. He expelled a peaceful sigh. These were the moments he cherished the most.

"I'm just doing what mom asked me to do," she said.

Caleb furrowed a brow at her comment and pulled her back so he could look at her more closely.

"What do you mean? What did mom ask you to do?"

Hope smiled up at him. "Before she went to be with Jesus, she asked me to make sure you weren't sad all the time after she left. She wants you to be happy, and I want you to be happy too."

Caleb didn't know what to say. There were so many different emotions swirling through his heart and mind, he felt overwhelmed and unsure if he could even speak at all. He had no doubt Abigail did just as Hope described. She was always thinking about other people instead of herself, even in her darkest hours.

Hope kissed his cheek before going back to her bedroom, but Caleb kept his place. He couldn't sleep even if he really wanted to. He thought a lot about Abigail's wishes and perhaps she was right. Maybe it *was* time for him to be happy again. Although he had everything a man could possibly dream of – his faith in God, a nice home, a good paying job, and a healthy child – there was still something missing and he knew what that was. It wasn't just the physical closeness with a woman he missed. More than anything else, it was the companionship shared between two people who love each other that he missed the most.

Caleb looked out the kitchen window over the sink as the sun prepared to make its debut. He knew the steps he needed to take to have that again, but he worried he might be too rusty to give it another try. After all, it had been many years since he courted a woman.

Caleb propped his elbows on the kitchen table, laced his fingers together, and bowed his head in prayer. *Lord, you know what's on my heart and my mind. I pray for your strength and guidance and for your will to be done in mine and Hope's lives. Amen.*

* * * *

Anna closed her songbook and laid it in her lap as the Bishop took his place behind the podium to preach. She glanced quickly around the crowded room to see who was in attendance, and it looked as if everyone from their small community was there. Church days were always day-long events amongst the Amish people, and Anna looked forward to seeing the friends she didn't normally see during the week.

"Someone is staring at you."

She looked to her left at her close friend, Karen, who whispered in her ear. She followed Karen's gaze to a far corner of the room where Caleb Roth was sitting. Hope sat beside him, but instead of watching the Bishop, his eyes were on her, and they didn't waver when she caught him staring at her. It felt like a battle of wills, waiting to see who would look away first, and she didn't know whether to feel excited or afraid.

He didn't look angry. It was hard to tell exactly what emotion was dancing across his handsome face. He was a difficult man to figure out. When the Bishop cleared his throat, obviously for her attention, Anna tore her gaze from Caleb and put her focus where it should be, on the Bishop's sermon.

When Karen giggled, Anna elbowed her in the side to make her stop. The heat rose to her cheeks, and when the Bishop turned back to his sermon, she vowed then and there to stop fretting over Caleb Roth. What good could come of it anyway? *Yah*, he was a handsome, hardworking man, but his heart was still bound to a cemetery plot on the outskirts of town and that would probably never change.

After the service, the women began preparing for the noon meal while the men set up tables and chairs beneath a large grove of oaks trees beside the church. Anna was thankful for the reprieve, and she kept her eyes on the task at hand and didn't let anything deter her.

When the meal was ready, and the Bishop gave thanks, she sat at a table with Karen and two other single women from their community. Several of the children she taught in school stopped by her table to say hello, including Hope, but Anna noticed right away Caleb wasn't with her, and that bothered her more than she would ever admit to.

After the meal, when the food was put away and the tables were cleared, everyone started making their way inside the church once again for the Bishop's afternoon sermon. As Anna walked beside Karen, she felt someone tap her on the shoulder, and her heart skipped a beat, hoping it might be Caleb, but it was Gabriel Conrad, a single father to two of her students.

"*Guder nammidaag*, Miss Brenneman."

Karen gave her a sly wink before leaving her side to join the others in the church.

"*Guder nammidaag*, Mr. Conrad. How are you?"

He took off his hat and held it with both hands.

"I'm doing well. Thank you."

He looked positively frightened, but she had no idea why. She noticed his three children standing several feet away, and they all smiled and waved to her, but they kept their place.

"Mr. Conrad, is something wrong?" she inquired. "Are the children having problems with their schoolwork?"

He shook his head and she noticed his forehead was covered in tiny beads of perspiration. He swallowed and cleared his throat.

"Oh no, no. They're doing great," he replied. "I was just wondering...I wanted to ask if you would like to have dinner with me sometime."

To say Anna was stunned would be an understatement. It wasn't that she didn't appreciate his offer, but he was several years older than her, so his invitation surprised her. His oldest child had already completed school and his youngest two weren't far behind. Still, she hated to be rude and decline, especially since it was obvious it took a lot of courage for him to ask in the first place.

"That would be nice. Thank you," she replied.

He seemed extremely relieved by her answer, and as they fell in step with each other and briefly discussed a day and time on their trek to the church, she noticed Caleb standing at the top of the wooden steps leading to the front door. He was watching her intently, but she didn't acknowledge him when she walked by and he didn't attempt to do the same.

Maybe it was better this way, since she'd already made a bad impression and caused enough trouble with him. As she and Gabriel parted ways, and she took her seat beside Karen, she couldn't shake the empty feeling deep inside her heart. Something was missing and she didn't know what. Perhaps she never would.

* * * *

Caleb sat atop his wagon and stared at the schoolhouse. It was the last day of school, and it also felt like his last chance. After today, he wouldn't see Anna every weekday, and that thought had a grip on his heart he couldn't shake. He would only see her a couple of times a month at church unless he found the courage to speak up now before it was too late...which it very well could be.

When the front doors opened a few minutes later, and the kids ran outside jumping and rejoicing over the beginning of their summer break, he smiled when he saw Hope ambling her way over to him. Caleb jumped down from the wagon and met her halfway.

"I'm surprised you aren't celebrating with the other kids," he said.

Hope glimpsed their way and shrugged her shoulders. "They may be happy, but I'm going to miss school."

She looked so pitiful when she said it, and Caleb picked her up and gave her a big hug before setting her feet back on the ground.

"Sweetie, would you mind staying out here a few minutes while I go talk to Miss Brenneman?"

Hope's sad frown turned upside down and her face lit up.

"I'll be on the swing!" she yelled, before darting off in the direction of the tire swing hanging from a pine tree beside the school.

Caleb climbed the steps and took a long, deep breath before opening the front door. He expected Hope to be alone, but two of her students lingered behind the others, and she was sitting at her desk, showing them something in a textbook. She looked up when the door opened, and she gave him a halfhearted smile before turning her attention back to the students.

He sighed. This was going to be harder than he imagined. She was obviously still angry over their confrontation at his house, and he wondered if they would ever be able to get past it. He walked slowly around the room, admiring the children's artwork tacked to the walls and trying to look busy. When her students finally left, the small space became so quiet you could hear a pin drop. Anna stood and walked over to the blackboard.

"Can I help you with something, Mr. Roth?"

He rolled his eyes heavenward. They were back to formalities again. He made his way over to her and stood patiently by as she erased the board. She looked so beautiful in her long blue dress. Her hair was gathered into a bun on top of her head, but several tendrils had escaped and now caressed her cheeks and neck. He took off his hat and gripped it hard with both hands so he wouldn't be tempted to touch her. The longing he'd felt for her since their first meeting stirred deep inside him, and he swallowed hard to try and remain calm and collected.

"Anna, please look at me."

She stopped and put the eraser down, but she didn't turn to face him right away. When she did, he noticed her expression had grown softer and she even smiled at him.

"I need to apologize," he began. "I shouldn't have spoken to you the way I did when you came to my house to ask about Hope. I'm thankful for your concern for her, and I'm sorry for my behavior."

Anna hung her head and shuffled her feet against the wooden floor.

"You shouldn't apologize to me, Caleb. I should be the one apologizing. I was angry during the drive to your house, and I should have waited and found out the facts before I started jumping to conclusions. You were right...about everything."

He looked out the window at Hope playing on the tire swing and he smiled.

"I asked Hope a little while ago why she wasn't celebrating being out for summer break like the other kids were doing, and she said it was because she's going to miss school, but what I really think she meant is she's going to miss you. I have to admit that the thought of not seeing you as often bothers me too."

She looked up at him, and it was obvious by her expression that his comment surprised her. He placed his hat on top of her desk and closed the gap between them.

"Am I too late, Anna?"

She tilted her head and gave him a curious look. "Too late for what?"

He reached out and held one of her hands, and he marveled at the softness of her skin. He also smiled when he noticed the effect he was having on her when he felt her body tremble.

"Is it too late for us to create a new beginning? To pretend that our misunderstanding never happened and start over?" he asked. "I saw you talking to Gabriel Conrad a few days ago, and I don't want to interfere if there is something between the two of you."

Anna laughed softly and shook her head. "There's nothing to interfere. We had one date, and I quickly realized we weren't mean to be together, but we parted as friends."

He tried not to let on how relieved he was by the news, but it felt like a huge burden had been lifted from his heart. Since seeing the two of them talking at church, he hadn't been able to concentrate on anything else. He knew Gabriel Conrad very well. He was searching for a wife to help raise his three children, and Caleb had the feeling it didn't matter to Gabriel whether they were compatible or not. He wanted a maid and cook – not a helpmate and companion. He felt the need to warn her, but he also knew it wasn't his place to stick his nose where it didn't belong, so instead he prayed fervently for her to come to the same conclusion herself, which apparently, she must have.

"Does that mean we can officially start over then?" he asked.

When she nodded in return, he let go of her hand and took a few steps back. He grabbed his hat from the desk and put it back on before clearing his throat. He tipped his hat to her and smiled.

"Hello, Miss Brenneman. My name is Caleb Roth. It's so nice meeting you."

He reached out and took her hand, and when he brought it to his lips, he tried not to grin when he noticed how her bottom lip quivered.

"It's nice meeting you too, Mr. Roth, but please call me Anna."

He stepped closer until there was barely enough space left between them to breathe. He could detect a faint whisper of lavender in her hair and on her skin, and he breathed in deeply, savoring the scent.

"Anna," he whispered. "Would you please do me the honor of letting me take you out on a date?"

He didn't know if it was the closeness of their bodies that made her unable to speak or something else, but she blushed before nodding. Happiness flooded his heart, and perhaps he was taking a risk, but he wanted to kiss her so badly, and he knew if he didn't he would lose his nerve.

Caleb brushed his fingertips against her cheek before leaning over and briefly pressing his lips to her own. It may have lasted only a few seconds, but the impact of it lingered as he felt a surge of heat rush through his veins and warm his blood. Every part of his body ached to kiss her again, only this time more earnestly, but he also didn't want to risk scaring her away, so he moved away from her slightly to try and ease the temptation.

Suddenly the front door burst open and Hope was running toward them. At first, it frightened him, thinking something must have happened to her while she was outside, but when she drew closer, he noticed the enormous smile on her face.

"I saw it!" she exclaimed. "I saw you kissing!"

Caleb sucked in a breath, having totally forgotten she was right outside the window on the tire swing. He glanced at Anna, who also looked very nervous.

"Does this mean I'll be seeing you a lot this summer?" Hope asked.

Caleb and Anna exchanged a knowing glance.

"Would you be okay with that?" Anna replied.

Hope clapped her hands together excitedly and ran behind the desk so she could wrap her arms around them both. "Yes!"

Anna stood on her tiptoes so she could whisper in Caleb's ear.

"It looks like you have yourself a date, Mr. Roth."

He kissed her forehead and grinned. "And I hope it's the first of many."